A MURDEROUS AFFAIR

LADY KATHERINE REGENCY MYSTERIES BOOK 4

LEIGHANN DOBBS
HARMONY WILLIAMS

SUMMARY

Lady Katherine juggles Christmas festivities, a perplexing cold case and a wager with the annoying Captain Wayland that will prove once and for all which of them is the better detective.

It's the Christmas season in London, but the holiday festivities don't deter Lady Katherine from investigating a death that happened months earlier. Since the victim was a maid, investigative resources were sparse, and the police hastily wrote it off as a random killing. But Lady Katherine and her friends believe it was nothing short of premeditated murder, and they vow to seek justice.

With her Bow Street Runner friend Lyle acting as a neutral party, Katherine teams up with her friend Prudence Burwick, her maid, Harriett, and of course her pug, Emma. Wayland has the aid of Pru's fiancé, Lord Annandale, and his valet McTavish.

The two teams race against each other in a hunt for

clues that takes them through the servants' quarters, stables, and seedy underbelly of London in search of a dangerous killer who thinks they got away with murder.

Will the best men... or women... win?

CHAPTER ONE

Thursday, December 26, 1816.
Mayfair, London.

THE WINTER CHILL seemed to have embedded itself in Lady Katherine's bones by the time a man answered Lord Annandale's door. Having expected the Marquess himself, she stopped short and blinked up at his overly large, shaggy, ginger-haired valet. No small woman, Katherine hadn't yet gotten used to looking up to meet the gaze of so many men.

McTavish grinned and waved her inside. "Come on in, lass, before you freeze your delicates off."

The last time she had come here, he had made a

vague reference to her *peaches*. She didn't know whether "delicates" was an improvement or not.

Trying not to take the outlandish greeting personally, she stamped her feet free of snow and skirted inside. Her pug, Emma, scampered inside without any such care to the dirt she tracked. Katherine tried to rein her in circles around the front mat to dry her paws a smidge.

"It's St. Stephen's Day. Shouldn't you have the day off?" Her lady's maid, Harriet, had been given a free day, along with the household staff in Katherine's father's, the Earl of Dorchester's, London townhouse. The family was supposed to fend for themselves for this one day while the servants visited their families for the Christmas season.

McTavish shrugged his broad shoulders. Even though he was dressed impeccably in Annandale's livery, he cultivated an air of barely contained ferocity. It was an edge that Lord Annandale shared, himself. But Katherine's closest friend, Prudence Burwick, didn't seem to mind the air of wildness in her fiancé — and he undoubtedly cherished her blunt tongue and no-nonsense attitude. Neither might fit the conventional image, but Katherine was far from conventional, herself. She'd come to adore them both.

"Och now, all my family is in Scotland. Who would I visit here in London?"

He had a point, there. At his insistence, Katherine doffed her pelisse and handed it and her gloves over to his care. He stored them away and ushered her up the steps.

"Off you go now, lass. You know the way." He winked.

Katherine hesitated for only a moment before she tugged on the leash in her hand, herding her pug farther into the house. Emma paused to shake her fur free of fallen snow before preceding Katherine up the stairs. The click of her claws echoed in the relative stillness of the house.

When she found the drawing room, Katherine paused in the entryway to assess her surroundings. The cozy room had changed since they'd first started meeting here. From somewhere, Lord Annandale had found a paisley-patterned sofa to squeeze between the over-stuffed armchairs. Between the furniture and the ever-green boughs trimming every available surface, there was scarcely room to move when the room was empty. Now, it was packed full, Katherine the last to arrive.

As Emma yipped, announcing their presence, the hum of conversation stopped. The plush rug underfoot muffled Emma's footfalls as she strained against the leash, aiming directly for the one person in the room Katherine did not care to meet.

Captain Dorian Wayland monopolized one of the armchairs, his long legs stretched out in front of him and crossed at the ankle. As Emma continued to tug at her leash, Katherine dropped it. The pug trotted up to him with unrestrained glee. Wayland, for his part, set aside the tumbler of spiced amber liquid he held. Depositing it on the table in the midst of the gathering with one hand, he leaned down with the other to give Emma a hearty scratch.

"I see you've been thinking about me, haven't you?"

Although his fingers sifted through Emma's fur, his gaze was firmly on Katherine. For a moment, she was struck dumb, thinking the comment was aimed at her. *Don't be ridiculous.* Since he'd returned to London from an extended stay in Scotland with Lord Annandale, Wayland had scarcely given her the time of day. He'd contributed to the last mystery she'd solved simply because he'd had the bad fortune to have been visiting his friend every time she arrived to discuss the case.

Was that his excuse today? Surely he, like her, had family engagements to devote himself to attending.

She'd left her house amid the protests of her sisters, who had arrived with their families to make the boxes of goods to take to the less fortunate today.

With a fond smile, Wayland applied himself to stroking Emma with his long fingers. She scowled. Of course he would address her dog rather than her. With a huff, Katherine pretended not to notice the slight. She turned away from her pug to greet the others in the room. For all she cared, Emma could crawl into his lap.

Traitorous, shameless dog.

Lord Annandale, the host, was conspicuously absent from the room. His fiancée, and Katherine's dear friend, Prudence Burwick, perched on the edge of the sofa. A wide swath of space rested between her and the sole other man in the room, who leaped to his feet at her arrival.

Despite the difference in their stations, Lyle Murphy — an officer at Bow Street — portrayed far better manners than Captain Wayland, the heir to a viscount. Bald relief etched across Lyle's freckled face, as long and narrow as a lanky form. He beckoned her closer to sit between him and Pru. Katherine had to step over Wayland's outstretched legs, between him and the skirts of the woman occupying the elegant chair with its back to the door.

"I'm pleased you could attend, Lady Katherine."

The remark came not from Lyle, but from the woman facing the sofa. Dressed in elegant, rich blue, Lady Lucy Brackley clasped a squat, leather-bound tome between her fingers. Although not yet thirty, a thread or two of gray had started to creep into the dark hair at her temples, reminiscent of the sharp streak of white her brother, the Duke of Tenwick, sported. She tapped the edge of her notebook on her knee, seeming impatient.

Caught between her shrewd gaze and Lyle's frown, Katherine wondered how long the marchioness had been hounding him for the details of his life. Lady Brackley was constantly on the hunt for more information to use in the novels she penned. In fact, Katherine suspected she attended the meetings of the Royal Society for Investigative Techniques, where they had met, simply to learn of more fodder. The marchioness could be relentless in the pursuit of knowledge, a trait which now glinted in her velvet-brown eyes.

"I see I'm last to arrive," Katherine said, keeping her voice neutrally diplomatic. "Forgive me. I would have been here sooner if not for a family engagement." With her stepmother, Susanna Irvine's, pregnancy, her father had opted to make this year's festivities even grander than usual. Never mind that she wasn't yet far enough along in her pregnancy to show. That fact didn't stop him or the rest of the family from celebrating what might be his and Susanna's last attempt to beget an heir. Although pleased for them both, Katherine had come to yearn for peace and quiet — not to mention a haven from her parents' constant cooing. They acted like newlyweds all over again! Katherine had been old enough upon his remarriage to remember.

Pru leaped to defuse the tension in the air. "You aren't terribly far behind Wayland. Don't think on it."

Katherine would prefer not to think of herself and Wayland in the same sentence. Thank goodness her father was too deep in celebrating to investigate the company she kept these days. The very last thing she wanted was to face censure from him over occupying the room with his rival, a detective he loathed...though Katherine hadn't yet discovered why. Yes, Wayland could be arrogant and crafty, but aside from nearly kissing her and then utterly ignoring her, Katherine couldn't pinpoint what about him was so thoroughly loathsome as to spark her father's undying enmity. He certainly hadn't done those things to the Earl of Dorchester.

As for herself... Her gaze strayed to his figure, where he bent over Emma and unrepentantly gave her the attention she craved. No, Katherine had best not think of him at all. If her father disliked him, that should be good enough for her. Even if he was a rather good detective.

Shifting in her chair, Lady Brackley jostled her notebook to a faster beat. "Yes, Christmas and all. It is a crying shame that we haven't been able to meet to discuss this sooner."

Next to Katherine on the sofa, Lyle shifted his weight. He plucked at the collar of his jacket. "I'll have to accept the blame on that account, my lady. It's been so long since the date of this murder you asked us to investigate that I've had difficulty finding information."

Lady Brackley stilled, tucking her notebook closer to her person. She smoothed her expression the same way she did her skirts. "I can't allow an upstanding gentleman like yourself to take the blame. Perhaps I'm frustrated for no good reason. Please, do tell what you've found."

Wayland paused his ministrations and sat straight. Annoyed, Emma rolled onto her back in his lap. He didn't appear to notice, resting his hand on her belly. "I'm sure if you wait a moment more, Annandale will return at last."

His voice was far too interested to account for him

happening to have visited his friend today. Tarnation! Who had invited him to investigate?

Most likely, Lord Annandale. Who in turn must have been told of the matter from his fiancée. Katherine couldn't fault Pru in wanting to apprise her future husband of the matter, especially not when he had developed such a desire to participate. However, no one seemed to listen to Katherine when she protested Wayland's involvement. Even Lyle, her longest friend, had taken a shine to the scoundrel.

Muttering under her breath as she shifted on the seat, Pru seemed distressed. "What is taking him so long?" The downturn of her mouth accentuated her sharp chin and nose. She plucked at her skirts, ill at ease. Although not as wide in the hip as Katherine, she was sturdily built, and squashed between her and Lyle, Katherine felt every miniscule change in position.

"I'm sure he'll be along shortly, like Wayland said." Although she loathed having to agree with him outright, she didn't like seeing Pru distressed.

A crinkle formed between her friend's eyebrows. "Perhaps I should have offered to help."

At that moment, Lord Annandale — as tall and wide in the shoulders as his manservant, though Lord Annandale's hair was auburn rather than ginger, and he kept a neatly groomed beard — sidled into the room with McTavish on his heels. "I would not hear of it, lass. You'll be the lady of the house someday, but until you set your heart on a wedding date, I'll do for myself."

The brunette's cheeks turned cherry pink, and she looked at her knees, a smile teasing at her lips. To give her a moment to compose herself, Katherine turned her attention to the tray Lord Annandale cradled between his hands. She raised an eyebrow as he set it on the low table and busied himself overturning the cups. Had he cleaned out the larder? He'd piled everything imaginable on the tray, from pickled eggs to seedcake. Katherine heartily prayed he hadn't been left to his own devices to fix the tea.

When McTavish stepped forward to serve the group, Lord Annandale glared at him. "It's your day off, you brute. Sit down."

Not that McTavish had anywhere to sit, unless he cared to squeeze onto a foot stool.

Lady Brackley tapped her notebook over her mouth. Katherine couldn't tell whether she attempted to withhold a smile or frown. However, she — like all the Graylocke siblings — was far from conventional herself. Katherine doubted that she minded the relaxed manners employed by Katherine and friends.

If she had, she would never have beseeched them to investigate this murder.

However, now that everyone concerned was in the room, Katherine was eager to conclude this meeting. She had been forbidden to allow her extracurricular activities to interfere with this year's Christmas festivities.

Fortunately, Lyle appeared to be of the same mind as her. He straightened his cuffs and announced, "I hope you don't mind my bluntness, but I'm expected home by midday. Would you mind if I share what I've learned of this case for you?"

All eyes turned to Lady Brackley. Since she had hired their services in the name of filling in the blanks for a new novel she penned, they deferred to her. Privately, Katherine hoped she would also employ the group to read her new book before it was published. Lady Brackley's books were nothing if not entertaining, and Katherine loved a good mystery. She wouldn't mind testing her intellect against that of a woman who a decade ago had been pivotal in the apprehension of an infamous French spymaster. Katherine, of course, hadn't learned of the debacle until well after the fact, after Lady Brackley had retired from spying.

The lady in question inclined her head with a grace

at which Katherine marveled. Sometimes, Katherine wished for such elegance. Although she was the daughter of an earl, raised in the same circle of etiquette as Lady Brackley, she'd never quite managed to embrace delicate little movements. Hers were perfunctory, a testament to her years dogging her father's heels as he investigated the most cunning crimes in London.

Now that she had earned her dowry and her independence without the inconvenience of having to marry, she wished she had applied herself better to etiquette lessons. They might come in handy — more so than tripping over herself and falling against her suspects. The rumors that had arisen from her investigation in Bath proved the inadequacy of that particular ploy.

"By all means, Mr. Murphy. Please, tell us what you've learned."

Ever polite, Lady Brackley didn't raise an eyebrow when Lord Annandale handed her a cup of tea and an eclectic array of vittles. She simply balanced it on her knee and settled in to listen. Katherine did the same, even if she had no intention of eating the eggs. She picked at her seedcake instead, her attention rapt on her friend.

As an officer at Bow Street — a Bow Street runner, as they were wont to be called, though Lyle disliked the disdain infused in that moniker — Lyle had access to criminal records that she and her friends simply did not. He learned of all murders and suspicious deaths that occurred in London — including that of Ellie Simpson, a maid in the wealthy Mr. Blake's household.

Lyle cleared his throat, plucking at his collar once more. Color flushed his cheeks as he found himself the center of attention. It was a position he found disconcerting when women were present, all save herself, Pru, and Harriet. Though Katherine had caught him a time or two becoming just as flustered at Harriet's teasing. Letting his gaze travel over the room, he began to speak to no one in particular.

"As you know, Ellie Simpson's body was found in an alley this past summer, six months ago. I'm sorry to say, it happened the same night when a terrible thunderstorm started the fire at the Hound and Ale Pub. The pub nearly burned to the ground. I'm afraid my compatriots were far too concerned with the fire that night to pay much attention to a maid."

"What balderdash," Lady Brackley exclaimed. Her tone implied she would have preferred to say something far less congenial. She drew herself up, her delicate features pulling together in an expression of rage. "Her death is ignored simply because she was a maid?

She deserves the same consideration as someone of high birth. A *life* has been cut short."

Pru, sitting closest to her, reached forward and patted Lady Brackley's knee. "No one here disagrees with you."

Lyle cleared his throat. "Certainly not. If anything, I'm ashamed that men of my ilk have elected to ignore the maid's death. I understand that money carries some weight, but we have a duty to uphold..." He shook his head and returned to the topic at hand.

Emma, who appeared to have gotten her fill of Wayland, jumped down from his lap and trotted over to Lyle instead. When she pawed at his calf, he leaned down to pat her idly on the head as he spoke.

"Here's what I was able to find out: Ellie Simpson was found in an alley approximately three streets over from the Hound and Ale. She was stabbed, and the notes indicated the weapon was a short, sharp object not found at the scene. With the rain that night, no one was able to recover much evidence aside from that."

Katherine leaned forward at the same time as Wayland. "How deep was the wound?"

At the same time, Wayland asked, "How wide was it?"

Katherine glared at him, then at Lyle, urging her friend to answer her query first. As another thought jumped into her head, she blurted, "Where was the wound?"

Wayland spouted that precise question at the same time. For a moment, their gazes met. He cocked an eyebrow, challenging. She glared at him, not certain if she ought to be pleased that their minds were of the same bent. He shrugged off her displeasure.

Instead of speaking, he raised a hand to indicate she should continue. Katherine might not have decided whether or not to trust his judgment, but he clearly had no qualms in letting her take the lead — for now.

Like her, Wayland was a member of the Royal Society for Investigative Techniques, which he had used ever since returning from the war in order to hunt criminals and keep innocents on this side of the English Strait safe. Unlike Katherine, his activities were far better known simply by the virtue of his gender. Although she was an earl's daughter, if High Society ever learned that she investigated murders for a living, her invitations to events would dry up. And, given that she often investigated crimes that occurred at these events, that would be disastrous to her career. So, unlike Wayland, she had to pretend to be a matchmaker.

Though she *had* done well with Pru and Annandale, who stood quietly behind his fiancée.

Katherine turned to Lyle, who seemed disconcerted to find himself squarely in the middle of her and Wayland, and resolved not to dwell upon the fact that apparently she would be working with Wayland for this murder investigation. Technically, should her father ask, she was not. She was working with Pru — who was working with Lord Annandale... who happened to be Wayland's closest friend. Unfortunately, Katherine wasn't very skilled at pretending. She felt Wayland's hazel eyes on her acutely.

He doesn't know everything. She bit her bottom lip. She would show him who the better detective was. For all his skill, *he* hadn't been investigating crimes since he was ten years old. She had at her father's knee... albeit in an advisory or observatory capacity for most of those years.

"How many stab wounds were there?" she asked Lyle, determined to have the last word.

Lyle fished a small leather-bound notebook similar to the one held by Lady Brackley from his jacket pocket. He hummed tunelessly under his breath as he flipped through equations and calculations until he came to a page punctuated by numbers. He read them studiously.

"The body had three stab wounds, each of varying depths. One, below her ribs on the right side, appeared to be a glancing blow. It was fairly shallow, less than an inch deep, and scratched one of her ribs. The next..." He flipped to the next page. "The next was deeper, nearly an inch deep, a long slice across her belly. The last..." He frowned. "Below her ear. An inch or so deep and less than that wide. It severed an artery. There were shallow cuts in her arms and hands, defensive wounds." With a sigh, he shut the book and tucked it away. "I don't have exact measurements, given that the body was turned over to the anatomy school by her sister, who it seemed couldn't afford the payment to bury the body. The corpse has undoubtedly been dissected by now."

Katherine frowned. She pulled a notebook of her own from her reticule to jot down the information. Only an inch deep? That was a short knife, indeed.

"Who is her sister?" Katherine asked.

"Sarah Simpson. She was out of work at the time of her sister's death but has since gained employment in Lady Lansing's scullery."

Hard work. Poor girl. Katherine dutifully jotted down the information.

Clearing his throat once more, Lyle wrinkled his long nose in apology. "That's all the information I was able to find. My compatriots deduced that it was a random act of violence, perhaps a robbery or simply a thrill killing. A woman such as she would have been in danger walking through those alleys alone at night."

Lady Brackley's lips parted. "That's it? That's all you can find? Surely someone would have heard her screams—"

Lyle tipped his head toward her, brushing his hair out of his forehead. "If not for the fire, no doubt someone would have. But between the noise of the storm and the onlookers battling the flames, no one has come forward as a witness. It's possible no one heard."

Sensing Lady Brackley's disappointment, Katherine gave her a confident smile. "We're no strangers to investigating based on little evidence." After all, their last murder investigation had involved what everyone had presumed to be an accident. 'We'll discover who killed Ellie Simpson, that I vow."

Although Lady Brackley appeared mollified, she asked in a small voice, "How?"

The lack of evidence was precisely why she had approached Katherine. If she had been able to piece together the murderer based on the evidence she could attain by greasing a few palms, none of them would be sitting in this room. This case required a more experienced hand.

Squaring her shoulders, Katherine stood to take charge of the situation. She crossed to the far side of the table, commanding everyone's attention — even that of her traitorous dog. At the movement, Emma trotted up and rolled onto her back, begging for attention. For the moment, Katherine ignored her, trying to maintain a professional mien.

"Our first step must be to speak with Sarah Simpson. Her sister will know if Ellie had enemies or if she was embroiled in the sort of situation that might have gotten her killed."

Pru nodded, satisfied.

The armchair creaked as Wayland straightened to his full height — fully four inches taller than hers. He used that height to his advantage as he stood over her. "You're speaking of a maid this time, not a gently bred lady. With her duties, she would have little time to visit family. Sarah might have lived across London from her, for all we know!"

"She didn't have a job at the time of Ellie's death," Katherine insisted, stepping closer. She refused to be cowed, certainly not by something as insignificant as his height. "Someone had to have taken care of her in some fashion. That would be Ellie."

Wayland shook his head. He would not be swayed. He looked past her to the others in the room. "We should begin where she was employed — with Mr. Blake. I'm certain Annandale and I can ask a few discreet questions around the club."

Katherine bristled. "Family is family, no matter how widespread. If something important was happening in Ellie's life, her family would know about it."

Wayland sidled even closer. "Her employer would know."

Katherine scoffed. "As if you know everything that goes on in your household."

He cocked an eyebrow. "And what would you know about my household? Have you been asking around about me?"

Her cheeks burned, but she refused to give him the satisfaction of answering him. Of course she hadn't spoken to his household. That would be uncouth.

"If you're so set that your approach will solve the murder first, then you wouldn't be averse to making a wager." She crossed her arms over her chest, staring him down. His eyes lit with unhidden interest, chasing a shiver down her spine. Had she crossed a line between them?

"A wager?" The words dripped from his tongue like honey. He smirked, the most infuriating expression that had ever graced the face of any man.

And it transported her to months prior, when they'd taken shelter in an alley from pursuit and he had been close enough that she thought he might kiss her. But he hadn't. And it was a darn good thing too, because she didn't want him to, truly.

But now, standing this close to him, close enough to smell the rich cedar of his cologne, clouded Katherine's thoughts. She took the smallest of steps back, though she refused to retreat verbally. "Yes," she snapped. "A wager."

"What do you suggest?"

"Twelfth Night is fast approaching. I assume that you've been invited to Lady Cabot's ball?"

He raised his eyebrows. "Hasn't all of London?"

Twelfth Night balls were potentially the most coveted invitation of the Season. In order to ensure attendance at hers, Lady Cabot had sent out her invitations in November for the event on January fifth. Everyone was abuzz with speculation over the entertainments for that evening.

Although Lady Cabot hadn't assigned them characters to play at her masquerade, costumes were mandatory for the event. Katherine would give her dowry to see Wayland brought low as one of the least coveted characters of the evening. Her smile widened, more satisfied than Emma was after filching bites of food from the table. Wayland met her gaze with a shuttered one of his own. He was right to be wary.

"If you truly think you can solve this murder before me, then you won't mind wagering your fate at the ball. Whoever solves the murder quickest will choose the costumes for the other person." She lowered her eyelashes, raking him with her gaze from top to toe. "I would so love to see you as the jester."

He didn't seem daunted in the least. His smile widened, making the dimple in his chin wink to life. "Oh? I think you'd make a smashing Lucy Leerwell. The rules for Twelfth Night are the same as ever, aren't they? You have to act like your character as well as dress like her?"

Katherine glowered at him, tightening her arms across her chest. As if she would ever act the loose woman, chasing any man who crossed her path in the hope of matrimony. What would people think if she suddenly turned an interest to courtship for a night? She'd fought dreadfully hard to win a modicum of respect as an independent woman.

Her fate didn't matter, because she would not be wearing that costume. "I will solve this before you."

"Before me and Annandale, you mean."

Behind him, McTavish straightened from the wall and protested, "Och now, what am I? I'm in this, too."

Katherine frowned at him, which he interpreted correctly as dubiousness on her part.

He shrugged. "I got a taste for investigating last time. It was mighty entertaining."

When Katherine wrested her gaze back to Wayland, he presented a hand to her. He wanted to shake on the deal — on their wager. Before she clasped her hand in his, she said, "Very well. But if you have Annandale and McTavish to help you, I'll have Pru and Lyle."

Lyle raised his hands in surrender. "Please don't put me in the middle of this. Christmas is one of our busiest times of year for crimes. I haven't got the time to investigate outside of my duties, but I'll help you *both* in any way I can."

Katherine gritted her teeth. When had her closest friend become so fond of Wayland? Although Wayland had earned Lyle's esteem by not stealing the credit for catching the Pink Ribbon Murderer a few months back — never mind that neither man had been responsible for that triumph — they hadn't become bosom buddies while her back was turned. Had they? Perhaps she didn't want to know how close to Wayland Lyle's loyalties resided.

Fighting a sudden burning in her throat, she

turned back to Wayland and answered, "Very well. I'll have Pru and Harriet to help."

He extended his hand once more. "Then we have a deal?"

Katherine clasped firmly, pumping it once, businesslike. As he released her, his long fingers skated over her palm, and she fought the urge to rub her tingling hand on her skirt. "You have a deal. And I do so look forward to seeing you play the fool on Twelfth Night."

His smile grew, though he didn't appear the least bit daunted. "We'll see. Don't think I'll make for an easy opponent."

"Don't underestimate me, either."

His eyelids lowered until he studied her at half-mast. In a low voice that barely carried to her ear, he whispered, "I wouldn't dream of it."

CHAPTER TWO

Katherine entered Dorchester House with Emma and Pru on her heels. The air smelled crisp, the warm scent of the Yule fire still burning. This year, Papa had gone out of his way to find the biggest Yule log possible. He and Susanna wanted a good omen for the child to come, and that began by burning a Yule log so large, it barely fit into their hearth. With luck, it would burn until the new year.

The house, like Lord Annandale's, was quiet. With the servants away visiting friends and family, the only people in residence would be Katherine, her father, her stepmother, and her half-sisters. However, when she'd slipped away, her older sisters and their families had been descending upon the house en masse. She'd expected to find the family still at home. Without them, the silence made the grand edifice seem little more than a husk.

Katherine tapped her feet on the edge of the door before closing it, sloughing off the last of the snow to cling to her heels. She pulled off her gloves but didn't bother undoing her pelisse. "I'll just be a moment. If Harriet is here, she'll be above in my room or hers. Then we'll put together a box and find Ellie's sister. I believe Lyle said she lived in town?"

Pru nodded. Having taken notes during their meeting, she pulled out her notebook and flipped to the proper page. She squinted. "Sarah Simpson, employed by Lady Lansing."

Lady Lansing didn't live terribly far from Katherine. A lucky thing, for they would have to walk the distance since Katherine didn't quite trust her carriage in Pru's hands. Lord Annandale had been teaching Pru to drive, but Katherine had yet to see the result for herself.

"Come on then, let's not waste time."

Katherine led the way up the stairs. On the first floor, they passed the sitting room, where the Yule log crackled in the stuffed hearth. The glow of the log lit the silhouette of a feminine figure curled into a nearby chair. Harriet? Katherine paused in the threshold.

When the figure moved, she recognized her for her

stepmother. Susanna had a blanket tucked around her knees despite her nearness to the warmth of the fire. She used the short, sharp end of an erasing knife to pick at the seal on a letter. Her finger hovered dangerously close to the knife's sharp blade, rather than the delicate ivory handle where it should have been.

"Susanna, are you unwell?"

Her stepmother looked up. Katherine's half-sisters had inherited her stepmother's dark hair and wide, winsome smile. Today, the latter seemed stiff. "Katherine, you're home." Her eyes widened as she looked past Katherine to Pru. "And you brought Miss Burwick. Give me a moment, I'll fetch a cold collation from the kitchen."

As she struggled to her feet, Katherine held up her hand. "No need. We won't be here long. I'm only home to see if Harriet has returned."

"Didn't you give her the day off?"

"I did, indeed. However, I forgot to provide her with her St. Stephen's Day gift before she left. I got her something special this year."

Susanna smiled. "I'm afraid she isn't here. I'm the only one at home."

Her words sounded bitter. Katherine frowned. "Where has everyone gone? It isn't like Papa to leave you alone."

If anything, that seemed to sour her stepmother's mood even further. "Your father has gone out with the girls to take the boxes to the less fortunate. He says it's too cold for me outside. He doesn't wish for me to endanger the baby." She glanced from Katherine to Pru, then gracefully lowered herself into the chair once more. If not for the way she clenched her hands around the blanket, letter, and erasing knife, she might have succeeded in portraying a calm demeanor.

"I've just walked from Lord Annandale's house. I'm chilled to the bone. He may be right."

Susanna wrinkled her nose in distaste. "I know he's right, but I don't like being treated like an invalid." She sighed, long and gustily, as she leaned back in the chair. The lines around her mouth gentled. "He means well. This baby is important to us both." She set aside the erasing knife and laid her hand on her stomach. Was that a slight swell? Katherine squinted, but she couldn't be sure.

Should Katherine sit with her until Papa returned? She worried her lower lip as she glanced at Pru, who looked as impatient as the dog dancing around their legs. They didn't have time. If they wanted to win this wager — and Katherine would relish proving to Wayland that she was the more cunning — they didn't have time to linger.

What if Ellie's sister refused to speak with them? A smile tugged at Katherine's mouth as she realized they had the perfect excuse to visit with her. She stamped down a twinge of pity, knowing she had to leave Susanna behind. "Do we have any boxes left? Pru and I hoped to deliver one today."

Susanna fiddled with the blanket on her lap. "If your father left any, they'll be in the larder. He and the girls have been stepping in and out of the house all morning." She waved her hand toward the larder, seeming to dismiss them before she paused.

"You and Pru don't intend to stay out long, do you? We have a full schedule this Christmas. There will be little time for investigating."

It seemed that she knew, without Katherine stating outright, what she and Pru were about. Did they have their intentions written on them somewhere she didn't know?

Katherine didn't like the hesitation in her stepmother's voice. Only a month ago, she'd solved the murder of one of Susanna's good friends. She thought that would have secured her abilities in the eyes of her stepmother, but it seemed that Susanna — even if she didn't say it aloud — did not approve of her activities as wholeheartedly as Papa did. The very last thing Katherine wanted to do was argue about it. She was on the cusp of moving out of the house. Then it would be none of Susanna's business what she did with her life.

"We can't have any engagements today. It's St. Stephen's Day."

Susanna pursed her lips. "Not today. But I hope you'll be home for supper. The family is taking supper at home tonight to greet the carolers. We have wassail in the kitchen."

"I'll be home for supper," Katherine promised. She could do that much.

Susanna nodded, turning her face away. "Then take a box. Perhaps I'll make up one or two more while you're gone. We must have something in this house that we can add to it."

As Katherine turned away from the door, her step-mother called out after her, "And put on a scarf. It's cold outside. I don't want you to catch frostbite."

Katherine balked for only a moment at the motherly advice, wondering at the abrupt change in Susanna's mood. Would this be her demeanor until the baby was born? Hastening her step, Katherine hurried to depart. She counted her lucky stars that she would never have to go through such changeable moods, since she neither intended to marry nor find herself with child. Her life's dedication was her detective work.

LADY LANSING'S Mayfair townhouse was dark and silent. For a moment, Katherine wondered if she and Pru wasted their time by venturing here. After all, it was St. Stephen's Day. If Sarah Simpson had any other family to visit, she would not be at the house.

At her feet, Emma craned back her head and whined. Clearly, she was wondering if her mistress had turned into a bird-wit. Katherine shook her head, gathering herself. She headed toward the set of stone steps leading down along the foundation of the house. The stucco sides of the townhouse gave way to less stylized rock, and finally, when the soaring stone passageway loomed over their heads, the steps ended in the doorway. It was a servants' door, out of plain view of any guests who frequented the lofty manor. Katherine rapped on the door and held her breath.

No answer.

Frowning, Katherine exchanged a look with Pru. "Perhaps I was wrong, and Sarah isn't at home."

Pru pried out her notebook and flipped to the page where she'd taken notes. "Lyle said Ellie Simpson had no other family. That means Sarah has none, either. Where would she go?"

"That, I can't say. But if you worked in the

scullery, wouldn't you want to leave for the day?"

Scowling, Pru leaned forward and knocked hard on the door again. The noise echoed off the rock enclosing them. She, for one, didn't appear wont to give up at the first sign of discouragement.

Katherine couldn't blame her. Although she was pitted against her fiancé, Pru was extremely competitive. In fact, that competitive streak had been what had drawn him to her to begin with. No doubt she and Annandale had concocted a wager of their own to sweeten the outcome of this investigation.

As Katherine opened her mouth to ask, the door was yanked open from inside. It revealed a short blond woman who greeted them with bleary green eyes. She glanced from one to the other, ignoring the dog between their feet.

"Are you wassailers?"

Katherine hadn't considered that tack. Given the season, they could have masqueraded as mummers or carolers to gain entry into the house. Instead, weighed down with the charity box, Katherine had little choice but to stick with her initial plan. She hefted the box in her arms higher. "We come bearing a gift for the scullery maids. Would Sarah be in?"

The woman narrowed her eyes. She didn't look as old as Katherine's twenty-five years, perhaps a year or two younger. It was difficult to tell with the weathered look to her face. She clasped a dry, cracked hand over the edge of the door. "You speak like a lady. What would you be doing carrying boxes to the servants of other households?"

She didn't have to elaborate. If Lady Lansing discovered her actions, it would be perceived as an insult. Employers were trusted to give gifts to their own staff. Likely, Lady Lansing had already done so. Katherine hadn't heard she was cruel.

Perhaps Katherine had been in such a hurry to outdo Wayland that she hadn't given this proper thought. She should have waited for Harriet's return, waited for a different day or thought of a better ruse. But she was here now, and she intended to go through with this. "Is Sarah Simpson at home or has she gone away to see family?"

At the question, the woman's eyes spilled over with tears, and she looked down, her pale eyelashes veiling her eyes. In a small voice, she confessed, "I don't have any family. Not anymore."

When Katherine looked at her closer, she noticed that Sarah's eyes were red rimmed and puffy, as though she had been weeping. Katherine's stomach twisted. Clearly, Sarah still mourned the loss of her sister. This would be the first Christmas they had spent apart. If Katherine didn't have one of her sisters... But she would still have the rest of her family to carry her through it. Sarah had no one.

Gently, Katherine held out the box. "Take it. A Christmas gift. No one else in the house needs to know. May we come in a moment?"

Without meeting her gaze, Sarah nodded and stepped back. "I have some wassail on the stove, if you'll wait a moment."

"I didn't come here for sustenance."

Sarah shrugged, wiping her eyes on her sleeve as she turned away. She slipped the box onto a tall table and bustled towards the stove. There, she ladled amber liquid into three tin cups. It smelled spicy and tart. When she offered one to Katherine, Katherine didn't have the heart to protest again.

"Thank you for the box," she whispered. "It's very kind."

Katherine felt like even more of a heel. She'd given the box only to gain entry and learn more about Sarah's sister. After taking a bracing mouthful of the spiked cider, Katherine decided that a reintroduction was necessary. She held the cup in front of her, watching as Sarah sipped hers with a lack of interest. The poor girl looked numb.

"You are right in thinking me a lady, but I'm not

here only to give you the box. I am Katherine Irvine, and this is my associate Prudence Burwick. We're detectives looking into the death of your sister, Ellie."

Sarah jerked up her head, turning as white as a sheet. She took a hasty gulp from her cup and set it down with shaky fingers. "You're looking after Ellie?"

Katherine nodded.

Recovering from her initial shock, Sarah scowled. "Why now, after all this time? I went to Bow Street every day and begged you lot to look into the matter. I knew it was not some simple theft. Ellie was careful, she would not have been walking in that alley alone at night."

Katherine exchanged a glance with Pru. "I'm afraid we aren't associated with Bow Street. We are independent detectives."

Sarah snatched up her cup and turned to fetch herself another dram. Without looking at them, she said, "I haven't any money to pay for that sort of thing."

"We aren't asking for payment. We're asking for you to trust us for a moment and help us find justice for your sister. Were you close?"

Sarah returned with a scoff. "She was my twin sister. Of course we were close. We spent every moment we could together."

Katherine curled her fist until her fingernails bit

into her palm, trying to use the pain to steady her against a surge of triumph. She had been right — and Wayland had been wrong.

However, since he wasn't there for her to lord the matter over him, she endeavored not to show her sense of victory. If Sarah was as close with her sister as she claimed, and no one at Bow Street had deigned to listen to her, Katherine might be able to solve this murder before the week was out. Sarah must have valuable information regarding her sister's demise. Katherine gestured to the stools around the table and took one.

"I have a few questions for you about Ellie. I don't want to dredge up bad memories, but anything you can tell us might help us find justice for her."

After a moment's hesitation, Sarah took the seat opposite her. Pru seated herself to Katherine's right, and Emma did everything possible to wrap her leash around the table's leg. She didn't appear to be choking herself, so Katherine left her to play.

"Do you know if Ellie was having any problems? Perhaps with the housekeeper at work or her employer?"

Sarah shook her head. "Of course not. Ellie was always cheerful and friendly, and she was no stranger to hard work. Why would anyone want to harm her?"

Katherine raised her eyebrows. Clearly, somebody had. "Why don't you tell me? Could she have run afoul of an angry lover perhaps?"

Sarah shook her head again. "She didn't take any lovers. Ellie was a good woman, she minded her business. And I would know if her thoughts about lovers had changed." Her eyes filled with tears again, and she clenched her hand around the cup. "We told each other everything."

"No one in Mr. Blake's house had any qualms about her work?"

"No. She was happy there, she'd even tried to find me work in the household, but Mr. Blake had no open jobs. Her master and mistress were nice, not like most." Sarah lifted her gaze, the glimmer of a smile haunting her lips. "Ellie even went around in the carriage!"

"She did?"

Katherine fought back a frown. When would a maid like Ellie Simpson have cause to go around in her master's carriage? It was not done. If anything, she might ride around in the boot if the carriage was destined for a particular destination, but she would certainly never do so alone. Katherine prodded, "Do you mean she sat up with the driver or in the boot?"

Sarah shook her head. "No, in the carriage. I know because I was down looking for a job, going door-to-door near the Hound and Ale Pub, near..." She swallowed audibly, then continued with a falsely bright smile. "I ran into Ellie. She was in a hurry and didn't have time to talk, but I saw her get into a carriage with Mr. Blake's insignia on the side. They must have let her use it to run an errand, to save her the walk."

Pru jostled Katherine with her elbow. She gave Katherine a speaking look. High society did not loan the carriages to maidservants to run errands. If Katherine had wanted to do so even for her beloved Harriet, whom she thought of not only as a maid but as a friend, her father would have forbidden it. Ellie must not have told Sarah the truth about that, but Katherine didn't say anything. It was clear Sarah thought they shared everything, but apparently Ellie had secrets she wanted to keep even from her sister.

"Those sycophants at Bow Street won't do a thing! I can't tell you how many times I've been down there. And when they released the body to me, I even found they had stolen her bracelet."

A bracelet? Katherine shook her head, trying to wrap her mind around the sudden turn in the conversation. "What sort of bracelet?"

"It was a silver band with a clasp in the shape of a heart. It even had a little ruby set into the center."

A silver bracelet, on a maidservant? Katherine

clenched her jaw. "Are you certain it was silver, not silver-plated?"

"Of course! It was silver through and through, and heavy, too. Ellie had to polish it all the time to keep it from tarnishing. But those Bow Street thugs, they filched it!"

Lyle hadn't mentioned a single thing about a bracelet of that worth in his report. If it had been there, he would have done so. If anything, the fact that Ellie had had some form of jewelry that had then been stolen lent credence to the investigators' assumption that she had been robbed. Pushing away her wassail, Katherine informed her, "If it was stolen from her, it certainly wasn't one of the men at Bow Street. They don't do that sort of thing. They are honorable men who serve their city well."

Sarah's green eyes snapped with fury. She jumped to her feet, though it made her look comically small compared to the height she had occupied when perched on the stool. "Just you wait here. I'll show you everything Mr. Blake and Bow Street gave me after they were done with her. Everything she owned in this world." With that, she stormed off farther into the house and up a set of stairs. The heavy clunk of her footsteps echoed through the cavernous house.

Katherine took the opportunity to bend down and

unwind Emma's leash from the leg of the table. She had half a mind to let her dog loose in the house to see what she could find. Perhaps this mysterious bracelet would show up somewhere. Instead, she held fast to Emma's collar and scratched her behind the ears. If she let her pug free, there was no telling what Emma would steal. For the moment, Lady Lansing had no idea that Katherine had gained entry into her house. And Katherine intended to keep it that way.

"Do you believe her?" Pru asked.

Katherine straightened, bringing Emma with her to perch on her lap. "I don't know. She sounds very adamant, but a maid like Ellie could not possibly have a silver bracelet."

Pru nodded. "That ruby must be made of glass."

Katherine would not be able to tell for sure without examining the bracelet, which was mysteriously absent. "Do you think it is Sarah's way of trying to gain recompense? When we arrived, I could have sworn that she was genuinely mourning. But this fixation she has on the bracelet — on what would have been her inheritance — leaves me with a sour taste in my mouth."

Pru nodded. "And we both know Ellie could not possibly have been using Mr. Blake's carriage. So are we wasting our time, listening to her spin a tall tale?"

Katherine frowned. "Maybe we are, maybe not. Let's see what she has for us."

Within minutes, Sarah returned with a small box very near in size to what Katherine had given her. She dropped it on the table with a loud thud. Then, opening it, she began to pull things out of the box. A faded blue handkerchief — in fact, several. At Katherine's guess, they might once have comprised a single dress. Sarah must have cut out the bloody remnants of her sister's dress to make these. A small, faded stain still edged one handkerchief.

To that, she added a small Bible, another dress — this one plain and worn — a pair of serviceable shoes, a pile of underclothes, a bracelet of braided scraps of embroidery thread, and what looked to be a delicate nightdress. Was that lace along the collar? Katherine snapped up the item, pulling closer. Yes, that was certainly lace, and the fabric felt like fine silk.

With the recent embargo from the war, lace and silk were ridiculously expensive and hard to come by. So precious and sought after that there was a flourishing black market trade on smuggled fabrics. Smuggled or not, these items were expensive. For Ellie to have this... Perhaps Sarah wasn't lying, and she'd had a silver bracelet, as well. It was just as plausible an item to find.

The next item, a small silk reticule with beaded decoration around the opening, made Katherine even more certain that Sarah might be telling the truth about the bracelet. The reticule was too expensive for a servant. And it also told Katherine something else. Ellie's death was not because of a simple robbery. If it had been, they would have taken the reticule.

Katherine held the purse up, noticing that it was water stained only on one side. "This was your sister's?"

Sarah chewed her bottom lip and nodded, then added, "It was empty. They probably flicked whatever money she had as well."

Katherine nodded. "It's stained on one side."

Sarah sobbed. "Yes. They said she fell on it. Her body shielded it from the rain."

Katherine stared at the purse. The stain must have happened after the body was discovered and the police moved it, which meant that Ellie was killed before it started raining. And before the commotion of the fire at the pub. Someone might have heard or seen something. They needed to go back to the area and ask around.

Putting the reticule back in the box, Katherine asked, "This bracelet you mentioned...?"

Sarah scowled and regained her seat. "As you can

see, it isn't there. And I know she had it, she came over to show it off to me."

"You said she took no lovers. But how could she afford the bracelet?"

Sarah looked aghast. "I told you. She worked hard and saved her coin. She could finally afford a few nice things for herself. She was going to buy me nice things too, when..."

A shadow fell across Sarah's face, and she looked down, not seeming to see the table in front of her.

Katherine looked back into the box, making sure everything was folded. Something on the nightdress caught her attention. She pulled it up through the neck of the dress and found a stylized M embroidered in white thread into the soft fabric. Why an M? Ellie Simpson did not have an initial beginning with M. Could she have stolen this? Or perhaps it had been a gift from a lover — whether Sarah believed it of her or not. Perhaps Wayland had been right after all, and Ellie hadn't told everything to her sister.

But even so, the trip to speak with Sarah had not been for nothing. As Katherine thanked Sarah and took her leave, she couldn't help but wonder if they had found a vital clue. Someone was getting Ellie expensive gifts... And maybe those gifts had contributed to her death.

CHAPTER THREE

Katherine held her tongue as she shut the servants' door. Around them, snow drifted down in fat flakes like softly landing petals. It had already obscured their footsteps in the stairs, coating them instead with a slick, fluffy white coating. Tugging upon the leash, Katherine led Emma up the steps.

At the top, Pru paused to examine the empty house. No remnants of light shone to indicate that anyone watched them. It was just past midday, but the thick swathe of gray clouds overhead darkened the sky. After a heartbeat ascertained that they were not being watched from Lady Lansing's house, Pru turned to Katherine and leaned closer. They were almost of the same height.

"Ellie Simpson was certainly not killed by some random murderer, no matter what the Bow Street Runners believe. This was no robbery — or at the very least, no thrill killing."

"She was murdered for a reason," Katherine agreed.

Ahead, a group of strangers filed from one of the townhouses and into the ruts left in the snow by passing carriages. She tightened her hold on Emma's leash, lest the pug get ideas. She loved people, and after the way she'd taken to Wayland, it was clear to Katherine that her dog wasn't the best judge of character. Keeping an eye on the crowd too far ahead to hear them — certainly a group of mummers out begging wassail or coin from door to door, given their jewel-bright cloaks — Katherine returned to the more important topic.

"A maid cannot afford a silver bracelet, no matter what her sister appears to believe. Clearly, she isn't the most practical of women."

"She has to know her sister cannot possibly have made much more money than she."

Katherine didn't know how much Lady Lansing paid her scullery maid — nor how much Mr. Blake had paid Ellie — but she knew Harriet's salary. At seventy pounds a year, Harriet was paid almost enough for two people, but it was the cost of keeping her rather than having her defect to one of Katherine's sisters. She adored Harriet and couldn't imagine trying to get on with another lady's maid.

"The ruby might have been glass," Pru mused.

"Perhaps."

They might never know the truth of the matter if they couldn't find the item in question. Pausing in the street and turning sideways to the approaching group of mummers, Katherine caught her friend's eye.

"What about the lace? Are you going to propose that there is a less expensive look-alike to lace hanging about?"

Pru's cheeks colored. "Certainly not. Did you feel how soft that silk was? It cost more than my wedding trousseau!"

Katherine scoffed, but before she said a word more, the mummers were upon them. Emma yipped happily in greeting as the dancing group of five encircled them. A woman caught Katherine by the arms, spinning her around with a whoop and a laugh. The others, three men and a woman, all with faces painted so gaudily, Katherine might never recognize them plain, fell over themselves in a comic tableau to gain her attention.

She didn't care for the attention at all. As she reined Emma in closer, Pru tucked her fingers into the reticule swinging from her wrist and tossed a few pennies from her pin money at them. They thanked her with elaborate genuflections before hurrying on down the street to the next house with a candle in the window, indicating there was wassail in residence. Katherine stood very still, the tension in her body leaving remarkably slowly as the snow swirled around them as their only companion once more.

"You're pretty with your cheeks pink from the cold," Pru announced. It sounded less like a compliment and more like an observation.

Katherine looked askance at her.

Pru laughed. "Don't look at me like that. You are! And I think you're apt to forget it."

Katherine shook her head. "It doesn't matter whether I'm pretty or not." After all, her crowning feature was not her face, but her mind.

"You need to grow more accustomed to male attention. For someone so astute, you can be remarkably daft sometimes."

How had the conversation travelled from murder to how attractive she was to the opposite sex? It was a topic she didn't care to discuss in the least.

However, Pru assessed her with shrewd eyes and shook her head. "Blue looks wonderful with your complexion. You ought to wear it more. It brings out the color of your eyes."

Katherine elected not to point out that her eyes looked more gray than blue. For some reason, Pru had taken it as a personal offense whenever Katherine chose to wear understated colors so as not to draw attention. As the daughter of an earl, she drew attention enough as it was, and she didn't want to be fending off the attentions of fortune hunters or others who wished the association with her family. The less men noticed her, the better.

"McTavish has noticed. So has Wayland."

Sard it all! Pru delivered the last three words with an unbridled air of smugness. That, right there, was precisely why Katherine chose not to wear colors that attracted attention. She didn't care whether or not she was tolerably attractive, and neither should anyone else.

More importantly, Katherine had neither the inclination nor the time to have this argument with Pru over the color of her pelisse, of all things. If it hadn't been a gift, she would have stuffed it into the farthest recesses of her wardrobe.

Deftly turning the conversation to a more appropriate topic, Katherine asked, "Do you think they would have noticed Sarah? If she and Ellie were twins, Ellie likely resembled her in some way."

Her friend hesitated a moment at the abrupt change in topic. As Katherine resumed walking, Pru let out a breath and followed. She didn't press the previous topic of conversation.

"Yes, I suppose they might have. McTavish, at least. Wayland's admiration isn't so easily earned."

Katherine ignored the barb. She checked on Emma, who happily romped through snow drifts almost as tall as she. Without looking at Pru, she continued the conversation. "The sort of nightgown Ellie had must have been worn for a lover. Why would a woman own such an expensive, delicate garment for herself?"

When she glanced up again, she found Pru as red as a plum. It would have been comical, if not for the fact that they were discussing a murder. Katherine, at least, was attempting to do so.

"I'll..." Pru had to try twice before she managed to speak the words. "I'll allow that you're likely correct on that front. Who, then, do you suspect has given her the nightgown and bracelet? And what about the purse? That looked expensive too."

Katherine nodded. "It would have to be a gentleman. No footman could afford such items any more than Ellie could."

Logic chased away Pru's embarrassment, and she nodded. "You're right. But wealthy men take maids into their beds all the time."

Katherine cocked an eyebrow. "Do you think they all give gifts of silver and lace to their mistresses?"

She had to raise her voice above the clamor a few houses down. Farther along the street, a troupe of sword dancers thrust and parried to an elaborate, choreographed show that looked more lethal than it was. They went out of their way to strike their flimsy weapons against one another's beneath the enthusiastic eye of the family in the doorway.

Since they didn't appear to pay any mind to the world outside of their audience, Katherine felt safe enough to continue the conversation. "We need to speak with a gossip. And we also need to go back to the area where Ellie was killed. The fact that the reticule wasn't wet means that she was killed before the commotion of the fire. Someone might have heard, and I want to question the shop owners."

Pru nodded. "A journey to that part of town can be arranged, but first, I know how we can speak with a gossip. Lady Dalhousie is certain to be at the ball tomorrow night."

As loath as Katherine was to speak with the vapid gossip, who cared more for theatrics than facts even if she knew the best stories that people preferred to keep hidden, she resigned herself to an evening spent fielding Lady Dalhousie's questions.

Just as she was about to agree, Pru volunteered, "I'll ask her."

Katherine's mouth hung open. That was rather selfless of her friend. Or was it? Pru's mouth tipped up in far too mischievous a smile for Katherine's peace of mind.

"You can occupy Wayland so he doesn't overhear what I'm saying. While you're at it, see if you can discover what they've learned without tipping our hand. You know I can't do it."

Katherine wasn't afraid of Pru's ineffectualness around Wayland so much as how much her friend might reveal to her fiancé. They were competitive, but he presumably knew her well enough to glean whatever he wanted from her.

On the other hand, Katherine had enough skill to evade Wayland's questions regarding her part in the investigation. She'd done it before a time or two, after all. Despite this wager between them, they were certainly not working together. And *if*, by chance, Wayland happened to be captivated by her eyes and

that caused him to tell more than he intended...
Perhaps Katherine would wear blue tomorrow,
after all.

NEWS of the family's good fortune — in other words,
Susanna's pregnancy — had spread far enough to reach
their usual chandler. This Christmas, he had gifted
them with a Yule candle so large, it had burned for two
nights and was now on its third. This, undoubtedly,
would be the last. Katherine heartily hoped the
guttering flame lasted for the rest of the meal.

By the light of the Yule candle, her entire family
was crammed into the dining room. Her father, the
light shining off the high forehead exposed by his
receding hairline, sat at the head of the table. Susanna
remained at his side, the place of honor at the far end
given to Katherine's maternal grandmother. A short,
shriveled old woman with a thick mass of white hair
and a piercing dark gaze that Katherine hadn't inherited, she was perhaps one of those most excited for the
new baby to come. Since the child would have no
blood relation to her, it had caught Katherine by
surprise. Perhaps she had simply grown tired of doting
on Elise, Katherine's eldest sister's, twin sons, now

toddlers, and looked forward to another infant in the family. Heavens knew she had been hinting at Katherine's second-eldest sister, Lydia, that it was time to conceive. Katherine doubted that Lydia's childless state was due to a lack of trying, for she and her husband loved each other with as much ardor as Elise and her husband.

Both sisters had been wed, with Katherine's help, to love matches. It was how she had gotten her reputation as a matchmaker. At her father's urging, she had encouraged it, as a means of concealing her true profession, which those of High Society would not understand. Although it was kept less a secret that he dabbled in detective endeavors, it wasn't openly discussed either. In Katherine's opinion, the lords and ladies of London were insipid dolts who didn't have a lick of sense or practicality. She played her part for now only because it suited her. Save for this particular murder, she had henceforth chosen crimes to solve that had occurred beneath the noses of these very lords.

Next to her, Elise picked at her plum pudding. Although all three of her mother's daughters had inherited her brown hair, and Katherine shared Elise's wide-hipped figure, Katherine had only her father to blame for her height. Elise, like Lydia, was far shorter. Even sitting, her head scarcely reached Katherine's ear. When a lock of her hair brushed against Katherine, it tickled.

Although they were midway down the table, with the children at the end next to Grandma Radcliffe and Elise's husband in between, her sister spoke in a low voice when she whispered, "Why doesn't she harass you to have a baby?"

"I'm not married," Katherine said smugly as she lifted a spoonful of the cake to her mouth.

"You could be, if you had the inclination."

"Which I don't," Katherine said, her voice final.

Fortunately, she was saved from having to continue the conversation as the sound of the knocker on the front door resonated through the house.

"Carolers!" exclaimed Maggie, Katherine's seven-year-old half-sister. "I'll get the wassail!"

As she raced from the room, Susanna leapt to her feet to chase after her youngest daughter. Her eldest, aside from marriage, trotted alongside her with an exasperated look that Katherine didn't envy. Connie was trapped in the realm between child and adult, not yet fifteen and yet too old to enjoy Maggie's antics.

The room erupted into chaos, the movement making the candle flame flutter perilously close to snuffing out as everyone — the earl, Grandma Radcliffe, Katherine's two elder sisters, their husbands, and Elise's twin sons — filed out of the room to answer the front door. Not yet done with her plum pudding, Katherine balanced her plate on one hand as she followed Susanna toward the kitchen, in case they needed aid.

When she arrived, Maggie was reaching up on her tiptoes to pull the pot of wassail down off the stove. Susanna lunged, steering her away as Connie offered her an armful of tin cups instead.

"Can I give out the cups to the carolers, Mama?"

"Yes, but I'll pour."

Susanna grabbed one handle of the pot, Connie taking up the other to carry it between them. The three looked so alike — differently sized, slender, dark-haired women with fair complexions and stubborn mouths — that for a moment, Katherine felt the outsider in her own home. Would the new baby share the features so prominent in her two sisters?

Then Maggie caught sight of Katherine and grinned in welcome. "Kitty, did you want to carry some cups?"

Katherine fought back a grimace. She hated being referred to as Kitty. Unfortunately, her youngest sister had decided that everyone's name had to rhyme. If Katherine recalled, there had even been a poem written.

The servants' door opened, spewing cold air and a billow of snowflakes. They gushed around the form of a woman with dark hair fighting her hat. Katherine smiled in relief to find Harriet at home again.

"I couldn't possibly take away from the most important task. You do it, Maggie."

Her sister didn't need to be told twice. She skipped out of the room, her mother and sister straining as they followed. The moment they passed, Katherine caught Harriet's arm with her free hand and towed her farther into the house.

"Quick, before they notice I've left. I've so much to tell you."

Harriet stumbled a moment, the air leaving her lungs in a wordless protest. At the narrow servants' stair, Katherine released her to climb ahead, aiming for the one room where they were certain to find privacy — her own. As they approached the door, the sound of the carolers below muffled by two floors in between, Emma scratched and whined from within. She hadn't been welcome in the dining room.

The moment Katherine opened the door, the pug burst into the corridor and launched herself at Harriet's legs, vociferously protesting her confinement. Harriet knelt in front of the pug to pat her head, then clucked her tongue. "What have you done with your ribbon this time?"

Katherine hid a smile. Instead, she stashed her plum pudding on the writing desk. She returned to pull Harriet to her feet and steer her inside. "Come. Sit."

At Katherine's urging, the maid took the vacant writing stool. However, she perched on the edge, looking at odds. Given the way she examined the tidy room, she must have expected to find it in shambles upon her return. Katherine liked to think herself a neat enough person to be able to clean up after herself for one day.

"How was your visit to your family?" Katherine asked as she crossed the room in search of the box she'd put together to give to Harriet. She listened to the answer with only half a mind as she searched. For all that she was neat, she apparently also had a talent for hiding things. She hadn't wanted her maid to happen across it should she return home early.

"It was very nice, thank you. But I'm more interested in hearing what Lyle had to say. It's a pity I couldn't attend both."

There. Katherine spied a suspicious lump beneath the cushion of an armchair she often used to read her notes in the evenings. She plucked off the pillow to reveal a box roughly the same size as the charity box she'd given to Sarah Simpson earlier. This one, however, was adorned by a jaunty green bow and a sprig of holly.

Beaming, she turned to present Harriet with the box. "I'll tell you in a second. First, open this."

Although she appeared to fight it, a smile crossed Harriet's face as she accepted the gift. "Thank you. But can't we do both at once?" She examined the ribbon, wrapped around the sprig, before she carefully tugged at the end. "It wasn't well done of Lyle to decide to hold the meeting on the one day I wouldn't be able to attend."

Had Harriet gotten a taste for investigating at last? That boded well, considering that Katherine had hoped to sweeten her up well enough to cajole her into helping. Without her, their team was short one member.

"He informed me that Christmas is a time of an unusually high number of crimes. I believe today was his only free day, as well."

After she untied the bow, she carefully set the ribbon aside on the table. Her gaze didn't leave Katherine's as she loosened the lid. Katherine felt as though ants danced along her spine, anticipation swelled in her so palpably.

"Well? What did he have to say?"

Stifling a sigh, Katherine turned to pace toward the bed. Emma reached it first and attempted to jump on. She nearly made it, but her weight dragged her to the floor once more. She grunted as she trotted away, as if the thought to join Katherine had never crossed her mind.

As Katherine lowered herself to the bed, she admitted, "He wasn't able to provide much information. It appears that the murder was dismissed as a robbery or random killing, given the location of the alley and the fact that she was no one of political import."

"That's madness." Harriet clenched her fists around the box. "They dismissed the murder simply because of her station? She deserves the same justice as anyone else."

Were those tears shining in her eyes? Katherine pretended not to notice as she approached once more, thinking to comfort Harriet in some small way. But what could she say? It was the unfortunate reality. If both she and Harriet were murdered, the men of Bow Street would spend far more time investigating her death than Harriet's.

"We all agree. That's why we've pledged to find

the person responsible and turn him over to the courts."

Harriet's gusty breath played along a wayward strand of her hair. She nodded solemnly and opened her gift. Her hand paused as she touched the fabric beneath, a summery gold swathe filling the box from corner to corner.

"I thought you must fancy it, seeing as you're forever trying to convince me to wear it. It isn't my color, but it will look smashing on you."

Continuing to pet the walking gown, Harriet whispered, "Thank you."

"That's not all in the box."

Harriet lifted the dress and found the jar Katherine had carefully tucked beneath it. Softly perfumed hand cream, for Harriet's skin. Whenever she handled lye, her hands cracked horribly and were wont to bleed if she wasn't careful.

"Thank you," she said again, equally softly. At that moment, she didn't resemble the wry, combative woman Katherine knew in the least. Concerned, Emma whined and pawed at Harriet's shoe. The maid set the box aside on the writing desk, snatched up the ribbon, and dragged Emma onto her lap to tie it neatly around her neck. That was more the Harriet whom Katherine knew.

"What else?" Harriet asked, her voice a bit more demanding than before. "Lyle must have learned something."

"She was stabbed with something thin, short, and sharp. No one heard any sort of struggle — there was a fire three streets over that night. I spoke with her sister earlier, but of course Wayland believes I'm wasting my time and he can do better."

Harriet pressed her lips together, looking down as she fiddled with the ribbon around Emma's neck. Emma looked about as pleased to be wearing it as a pig going to slaughter. "Captain Wayland was in attendance?"

By will alone, Katherine kept the disgruntled expression from her face. "He was. I gather Lord Annandale invited him." That was all she cared to say on the matter.

"And he told you he thinks he's the better detective?"

Harriet's eyes were twinkling with mischief. Surely she didn't agree with him, did she?

"Not in so many words. He said Ellie's employer, Mr. Blake, would know more of her personal business than her sister."

Harriet scoffed.

Katherine threw up her hands in triumph. "Thank

you! That sarding man doesn't have a lick of sense. I'd wager he doesn't know a thing about the personal lives of his servants. Well." Katherine frowned. "That wasn't precisely what I wagered, but that is neither here nor there."

After placing the dog on the floor, where Emma tried her best to rub away the ribbon by sliding her neck along the leg of the stool, Harriet raised her eyebrows. "There's a wager?"

"It isn't important. Would you like me to tell you what I learned while speaking with Ellie's sister?"

"Certainly." Although she pretended not to pay rapt attention to Katherine by reaching for the jar of lotion and helping herself to the smallest dab of the cream inside, Harriet held herself with a rigidity that belied the casual gesture.

Katherine perched on the end of her bed to continue the conversation. "Sarah seemed adamant that Ellie was a good, hardworking woman who would never take a lover. But she had both a silver bracelet — allegedly, it appears it has been stolen — a beaded reticule and an expensive nightgown with lace edging. She must have had a lover. Although..."

Harriet sat straighter, setting the jar aside. "Although?"

Katherine shook her head. "It's nothing. There was

an embroidered letter M on the inside of the gown, not Ellie's initial. Either she stole the item or perhaps M indicates the name of her lover."

"There is a third option," Harriet pointed out, though she did so while straightening the spoon next to Katherine's abandoned dish. "Are you going to eat this?"

"Not if you'll tell me what the third option is."

Her maid gave her a bright smile that reminded her of Emma at her most smug. She claimed the plate, digging the spoon into the dense, flavorful cake as she answered. "The nightgown might have been one of her mistress's cast-offs." She lifted the spoon to her mouth before using it to point at the box containing her gift. "Or had you forgotten that you gave me most of my clothes once you were done with them?"

Why hadn't Katherine thought of that? "I suppose it's one more thing to look into. I wonder what Mrs. Blake's given name is..."

"I could ask," Harriet said, drawing out her words. She helped herself to another spoonful of plum pudding. "I'm friends with the woman who does laundry in the Blake household."

Was there anyone in London whom Harriet was not friends with? Katherine marveled at her vivacious maid. "That would be splendid!"

"I'll ask her about Ellie while I'm at it, shall I?"

Katherine beamed. "Even better. Anything you can tell me could win us a step up over Wayland and his team."

"Team?" Harriet speared the cake. "So, there *is* a wager! What's the prize?"

"Not money, if that's what you're thinking. The winner gets to dictate what the loser will wear to Lady Cabot's masquerade ball on Twelfth Night." She clenched her fists. It seemed like such a trivial wager when she said it aloud, but her determination to outdo Wayland coursed far deeper. Due to his gender, Wayland already had access to people and places that Katherine did not. However, she would not allow that to daunt her. She *was* the better detective.

"And you've elected to form teams for this endeavor?" Harriet tucked another spoonful of plum pudding into her mouth.

Katherine stood, searching for something with which to occupy herself. Perhaps she ought to study her notes again or copy them out in a neater format. It might help her think. But Harriet occupied the writing desk, so she answered first. "Yes. Wayland will conduct his investigation with Lord Annandale and McTavish."

The clank of the spoon hitting the china and the

plate settling onto the desk surface jarred Katherine out of her frustrations. Harriet launched to her feet, her dark eyes glinting with determination and her wide mouth stretched thin.

"*McTavish* is investigating?"

Katherine hadn't thought it terribly far-fetched an idea, given that he had helped with the last investigation. She frowned as she studied her maid. "Yes."

"So it's he, Captain Wayland, and Lord Annandale against..." She trailed off, but when Katherine didn't answer, she guessed, "You, Lyle, and Miss Burwick?"

"No. Lyle's duties consume him too much."

"Three against two?" Harriet balled her fists. "That isn't a fair playing field. Tell Captain Wayland that I'll be joining on your side."

Katherine opened her mouth — she already had.

Raising her finger, Harriet added vehemently, "I am every bit as good an investigator as McTavish is. I'll be an asset."

With the raise of her eyebrows, Katherine said mildly, "After all these years helping me muddle through difficult investigations, I should think you are better than he."

"Then you'll let me help?"

"Let you?" Katherine tried hard not to betray her

smile. This couldn't have worked out better if she had orchestrated it. When had Harriet started such a vehement rivalry against McTavish? As far as Katherine knew, they were rarely in the same house together, let alone the same room.

It was a mystery for another time. For now, she contented herself by saying, "I would welcome your addition to the investigation."

Harriet grinned, triumphant, and dropped back onto the stool. She snagged the plate once more and tucked a large spoonful into her mouth. The morsel seemed too big for her to chew, because a curious expression spread over her face. A moment later, she spat a plain metal ring into her palm.

She stared at it, eyes widening. "What do you think it means?"

"I think it means that someone was bound to find it sooner or later." When stirring the plum pudding weeks ago before it set, the family had added the traditional charms meant to denote omens for the new year. Balderdash, every last one.

"No," Harriet said, juggling the ring between her palms as if it scalded her. "Do you think it's meant for me or for you? I ate it, but it was your pudding, so which of us will marry next year?"

"Neither of us. It's a silly superstition."

Narrowing her eyes, Harriet opened her mouth to argue. However, the earl's thundering voice pierced the air, calling Katherine's name. She smiled and excused herself, not wanting to discuss impending marriages of any sort. For once, the family's festivities this year arranged to her benefit.

CHAPTER FOUR

I f Katherine had had her own carriage — or better yet, her own house — she would not have been relegated to riding with her parents. Ordinarily, this would not have been quite such a challenge. She had plenty in common with her father and often spent evenings with him in his study, speaking of the particulars of difficult cases or playing chess. She and Susanna got along well, and she rarely foundered for conversation. But together, now that an heir might be forthcoming, the two had grown unbearably nauseating. If Katherine had to accompany the family on many more daytime visits — or nighttime events, as currently — she might start to grow morning sick along with her stepmother.

As the carriage rolled to a stop, Susanna pulled

away from the tête-à-tête with her husband and patted down the front of her gown, glimpsed beneath her fine, ermine-trimmed black cloak. "Do you think I look all right?"

The earl frowned, looking down at her with an assessing eye. What little light filtering into the closed coach emanated from the open window to the street outside. A streetlamp or a lamp hanging from one of the grand Mayfair houses. He made a humbling sound. "You have something right ... here." When he dipped to kiss Susanna on the tip of her nose, Katherine turned to look out the window.

The air cooled her hot cheeks. The pair of them were no longer newlyweds, but they might as well have been.

"Smile, Katherine," her stepmother prodded in a fond tone. "Or do you want my cousin to think you're a sour spinster?"

Katherine didn't give a farthing what Susanna's cousin thought of her, but she forced a smile none-theless. She loved her family, even if their behavior of late threatened to drive her mad. Soon, she would settle on her own residence and would begin to live her independent life.

The door opened, and Katherine waited for first her father and then Susanna to descend. Katherine accepted Papa's help in debarking, but the moment her slippers crunched into the crust of snow, she informed, "I promised Pru I would seek her out the moment I arrived."

With a frown, Susanna accepted her husband's arm, and they strolled toward the door of the towering townhouse, where a butler waited with the door half-open to let them in. "We have to greet my cousin."

"I will, of course." She would simply rather not do so with her parents and thus be drawn into more nauseating conversation regarding Susanna's condition.

Fortunately, the ordeal wasn't as painful as she anticipated. The hosts stood with their own grown daughter by the door to greet the guests. Susanna had no sooner said hello than the next pair of guests mounted the front stairs to be let in. There wasn't room in the foyer to linger, so they were directed down the corridor and into the three long sitting rooms which had been turned into a ballroom with the opening of the double doors between them.

Even better, the couple to enter directly after them was Lord Annandale escorting his fiancée. Katherine lingered in the doorway and caught Pru's eye before she entered the other room. She didn't have to wait long. Once she had given a cursory greeting to the hosts, Pru left her fiancé behind to engage them in conversation and joined Katherine in the makeshift ballroom.

The row of sitting rooms had been decorated in a way befitting of Christmas, with evergreen trimming the doorways, mantel, and windows, and holly and even Christmas roses arranged to the best benefit. Aside from the smell of beeswax candles, the faint aroma of cinnamon clouded the room.

The moment Pru reached Katherine's side — to one side of the main doorway where she hoped the fifty or so people currently in attendance wouldn't notice her for the time being — Pru whispered into her ear. "Have you learned anything else regarding the investigation?"

When would she have? Katherine could scarcely find a moment away from the Christmas celebrations to breathe, let alone investigate. If this ball hadn't satisfied both agendas, she wouldn't be investigating tonight, either. However, she and Pru had an agreement to exchange gossip with Lady Dalhousie.

Katherine hadn't yet seen the old woman among those gathered. Had she been there, Katherine would have undoubtedly spotted her at once. Lady Dalhousie was far from subtle. Aside from wearing the latest fashions, she never went anywhere — not even to the bath, as Katherine had discovered a few months past — without wearing her prized diamond and aquamarine necklace. According to Lady Dalhousie, the necklace had an auspicious lineage and had once belonged to Empress Josephine Bonaparte. Like most of the tales to exit the old biddy's mouth, Katherine didn't believe a word.

"Katherine?"

She turned her attention away from the mingling crowd and glanced at her friend. "I haven't. I've been occupied with family outings all day, and, it being the day after St. Stephen's Day, Harriet has had more chores than usual to contend with. She promised to help when she's able, and she knows a maid in Mr. Blake's household. Perhaps she'll visit tomorrow."

Pru sighed, her shoulders deflating. "Is that what has you so tense? I thought you had learned something else."

Tense? Katherine rolled her shoulders, relaxing them. She hadn't realized that she'd been holding herself so stiffly. She caught sight of her parents once more across the room. Susanna laughed, one hand lightly resting on the almost imperceptible swell of her belly while Papa bestowed a kiss upon her knuckles. He had been even more attentive than usual since learning of her condition.

Katherine fought not to make a face. She waved a hand toward the pair. "They've been doing that all day. No, all month. Cooing at each other like birds."

"Oh?"

The corners of Pru's mouth turned down, her chin jutting out as she surveyed them. While they watched, Papa put a hand to the small of Susanna's back and kissed the top of her head. She whispered something to him that made him smile as bright as the chandelier overhead.

"Do all married couples act that way when they're expecting an addition to the family?"

Having only her parents and her eldest sister to draw from, Katherine sighed. "Most likely. Elise and her husband were the same once she finally conceived. Perhaps he was worse. He wouldn't let her put on her own gloves without help."

Pru's eyebrows knitted together. "That sounds inconvenient. I wonder if I'll have to contend with behavior like that."

Katherine's eyebrows soared. "You haven't even set a date for the wedding! Are you already contemplating children?"

Pru blushed crimson to the roots of her hair.

She was saved as the next guests filed into the room. Katherine had never spoken at length to the

Marquess of Brackley, but she recognized him instantly by the vivacious, dark-haired woman he led into the room. They were followed by another young woman with raven hair, a telltale trait of the Duke of Tenwick's family. This young woman, dressed in a muted green gown with gold embroidery on the hems, looked a bit timid and demure. She kept her head bowed as she followed in Lady Brackley's wake.

As Lady Lucy Brackley spotted Katherine and Pru standing by the doorway through which she had entered the ballroom, she veered in their direction. Lord Brackley spoke quickly to his wife before they parted ways and turned to greet an acquaintance.

"Lady Katherine," said the marchioness with a broad smile. She touched Katherine lightly on the arm before turning to her companion. "Miss Burwick. May I introduce my cousin, Miss Honoria Graylocke?"

Katherine inclined her head to the young woman. "Lovely to meet you."

"And you."

The soft-spoken woman said nothing else and didn't seem appalled in the least when Lady Brackley turned the conversation to business.

"Have you had any luck hunting down that murderer?"

Katherine's esteem of the young woman increased

as she didn't so much as bat an eyelash. Perhaps Lady Brackley had discussed the inspiration for her latest novel at length. Or perhaps Miss Graylocke was made of sterner stuff than she seemed.

"Some," Katherine answered, once she had ascertained that no one was near enough to hear the conversation. "We visited the victim's sister yesterday, and I'm almost certain Ellie must have had a lover. I'm looking into that angle now."

Lady Brackley cocked her head to one side. "What makes you think that? She was unmarried."

All maids in the households of lords and ladies were unwed. It was a requirement of the job.

"She had a few items in her possession that would have made for appropriate gifts from a lover?"

"Oh?" Lady Brackley's eyes gleamed. Apparently she wasn't content with a mere summary of the matter. Should Katherine have invited her along? "Such as?"

Pru answered. "A bracelet and an expensive nightgown. There may be more, the sister told us of the bracelet, but it was not amid her things."

If anything, Lady Brackley looked crestfallen. "That's all you've learned?"

"Thus far," Katherine answered, drawing herself up. "Investigations take time. We won't be able to solve this in a day, but I assure you, we *will* solve it."

Her answer seemed to satisfy her client. As she nodded briskly, Lady Brackley's attention was immediately drawn by someone across the room. "Do keep me apprised. If you'll excuse me, I believe I see Phil. I haven't seen her since the last Society meeting. She's been out at Tenwick Abbey. I'm sure we'll speak again tonight." Lady Brackley nodded briskly and then tapped her notebook — which Katherine hadn't even seen her draw out of her reticule, since it was such a regular extension of her hand — on her opposite wrist. "Come, Honoria."

The young woman dipped in a brief curtsey and murmured, "It was a pleasure to meet you, my lady." She swept after Lady Brackley without another word.

At the junction of the two sitting rooms, the pair encountered two men and two women. One of the women, round with child, had a sweet, oval, freckled face and stood near to a man who resembled the Duke of Tenwick strongly, save for the brilliant streak of white in the duke's hair. The other woman was Philomena, Lady Tenwick, known as Phil to her friends. Katherine liked to count herself among them, so she waited until the serene, auburn-haired woman turned to her before nodding in greeting. The duchess returned in kind.

Katherine was so engrossed in the exchange that

she didn't notice another woman approach them until it was too late.

"So, you have your hooks into Tenwick's relatives, do you?"

Katherine stiffened, then turned to meet a woman approximately ten years her senior, give or take. Mrs. Fairchild — a woman whose husband never seemed to be present at the events she frequented — drew herself up even though she couldn't hope to match Katherine's height. The woman wore haughtiness like it was a cloak.

It took Katherine a moment before she realized to what Mrs. Fairchild, a rival matchmaker who had taken a particular dislike to Katherine, was alluding. "I am not matching Miss Graylocke."

Mrs. Fairchild cocked an eyebrow. "So you say, but we both know that you won't be able to resist the lure of such an auspicious match."

Katherine bit the inside of her cheek, but it did little to stifle her impatience. "I don't match my clients for status. I match them for love."

"So you say, but you managed to match this penniless bluestocking with a marquess. I wonder why you didn't hold out for a duke ... or a prince."

Katherine bristled at Fairchild's reference to her friend Pru. Pru and Annandale were the perfect match and clearly very much in love. Katherine hadn't even been trying to match them up! Even so, in Bath, Mrs. Fairchild's client had made the more auspicious match. However, Katherine didn't rise to the bait. If she aspired to be the most renowned matchmaker in existence, then perhaps she would have felt insulted. As it was, Katherine would just as soon have her peers forget that she had arranged matches for anyone.

Apparently Mrs. Fairchild had forgotten that both their clients had benefitted from the last match.

Katherine steeled herself, waiting for Pru to find her voice and tell Mrs. Fairchild exactly what she thought of her remarks. Luckily, before that happened, a masculine rumble sounded behind her. When he spoke, Lord Annandale's brogue was thicker. Katherine sometimes wondered if he did that on purpose to seem more intimidating.

"Och, now. That would nae be my future wife yer disparaging, would it? A foiner lass you would nae find." A challenge lingered beneath his words, full of menace. If Mrs. Fairchild had persisted in insulting Pru, Katherine doubted that Lord Annandale could have been roused to violence, but he might have come close. He was very protective of her, especially when she had her head bowed and her mouth pressed into a white line with shame and self-doubt.

Katherine clenched her fists but took even breaths.

To her credit, Mrs. Fairchild must have had some sense in her head, because she dropped the topic immediately. In fact, after a hasty excuse, she hastened to find whatever wayward charge she was chaperoning to tonight's event.

Lord Annandale sidled up to his fiancée, placing his hand on the small of her back as he leaned down to croon to her. "Do nae listen to her. You are the fairest, wittiest, slyest woman I could ask for, and there's no secret to why I fell in love with you."

At his words, Katherine's defensiveness melted away. She turned her back and took a few measured steps away to give them privacy. Truthfully, they were as bad as her parents with their cooing, but if it lifted Pru's spirits after such a heartless encounter, Katherine couldn't bring herself to resent them.

When she took a few more steps into the room, she found herself in the shelter of Wayland's shadow. He raised an eyebrow at her, assessing. Katherine met his hazel gaze boldly. She fought the urge to run her hands along her gown.

She'd worn a blue dress, as Pru had suggested. It was a muted shade of blue, the color of the sky with a thin haze of clouds on a summer's day, but it was blue nevertheless. Harriet had teased her to no end over the color but stopped when Katherine threatened to give her this dress, too.

Had Wayland thought her pelisse yesterday brought out her eyes, as Pru had? Why did she care?

Tarnation. She bit back the curse, realizing that Wayland had been staring at her for entirely too long. They were starting to draw notice. She hazarded a smile at him and prepared to step around if he wasn't going to say anything.

"Would you like to dance?"

Katherine turned back to him, narrowing her eyes. "I don't dance. You know that."

He shrugged. "I thought it might be as private a place as we're likely to get to exchange information."

This time, it was Katherine's turn to cock an eyebrow, though she doubted that she infused the gesture with as much arrogance as he managed. "What makes you think I care to exchange information with you? We're working against each other, or have you forgotten?"

A wolfish smile spread across his face, and he offered his arm. "That's never stopped me before."

True. It hadn't. A tremor washed over her hand. She fisted it. She wasn't afraid of him, nor did she think it likely that he would uncover anything about what she'd learned that she did not wish him to find.

"Not a dance, but I'll walk with you," she said firmly, though she laid her hand on his sleeve. For the first time since she'd come face to face with him, she noticed that he wore blue tonight, as well: a dark, sapphire-blue jacket that paired well with his black breeches. Had he worn that color on purpose? Katherine frowned at Pru, but her friend was still enthralled with Lord Annandale.

She shook her head. Why would Pru orchestrate for them to wear the same color? It would serve no purpose. As Wayland acceded to her wishes and took her along the perimeter of the small room, his pace leisurely, she shook off the suspicion.

When she spotted Susanna across the room — Papa next to her with his back turned — Katherine's hand convulsed. The moment Wayland felt it, he paused to look at her.

"Not here," she whispered, her words scarcely emerging from her choked throat. She kept company with Wayland so often these days that she'd forgotten for a moment how her father hated him! They couldn't be seen together. Panicked, she turned her face up to meet Wayland's. "In the corridor. There must be a card room set up?"

"There is, I imagine. Why are you so set on leaving all of a sudden?"

She leaned closer, lowering her voice so only he could hear. The muscles beneath her palm stiffened. "Papa is just over there."

He raised his eyebrows. "Yes, he is. Why does that bother you?"

"It should bother you," she bit out. "You despise each other."

The scoundrel had the audacity to smirk. "That's news to me. I have no quarrel with your father."

"Very well. He despises you. Does it matter if it's reciprocated? I can't let him see us together."

Wayland canted his head, a measuring expression on his face, but he changed direction immediately. He lengthened his strides until she had to lift her skirts to keep up. Only once they were in the corridor, away from the prying eyes of her family, did she slow her pace again. Her thunderous heart hammered in her throat painfully.

What in tarnation has gotten into you? This, if nothing else, was evidence that she could never afford to forget that Wayland was the enemy. If she started to trust him... it might be disastrous.

But she needed information from him, so she couldn't eschew his company altogether. He was a talented detective, if not quite as good as she.

"If all you wanted was a private moment with me, you only had to ask."

Katherine battled a scowl. Although she knew he said such a salacious thing to rile her, it worked. But she couldn't let him control the conversation, or she might let something slip about the investigation that she would rather keep quiet. So instead of delivering a tart retort, she looked up at him and smiled.

He blinked twice, and the arm beneath her hand stiffened. She paused in the corridor, prompting him to stop as well, and leaned closer.

"Perhaps that is precisely what I wanted."

He didn't say a word. Neither did he meet her gaze. In fact, he couldn't seem to decide where he should look. Over her shoulder, at her mouth, down the corridor. Her smile grew. She delighted in seeing him so flustered.

"Was it this easy finding a private moment with Mr. Blake? I assume you paid him a visit yesterday, as you proposed."

"Yes." The moment the word slipped out, he frowned. He threw his shoulders back as though donning armor. "He had several interesting things to say about Ellie."

"Did he now? Like what?"

"I'll tell you if you'll tell me what her sister told

you."

When Wayland leaned forward, matching her posture, Katherine realized she was far too close. She slipped her hand free of his arm as though scalded and stepped back.

"I don't think so." Her voice held far less conviction than it ought to have. She turned and took a halting step down the corridor before he caught her hand and laid it on his arm again, continuing the ruse that he was a gentleman leading a lady on a stroll through the house, rather than one of two astute detectives probing one another for information.

"Come, now."

His chiding tone was low. Katherine doubted it carried beyond her ears. For some reason, that made the heat climb into her cheeks.

"If you're so keen on discovering what I know, you'll have to give me something in return."

Should she pretend as though she had more information than she did, or less? She couldn't tell Wayland the truth. For all that they were investigating the same murder, he was an opponent, not an ally.

Pru had best be speaking with Lady Dalhousie. If Katherine was entertaining her father's enemy for nothing, she would wring her friend out like a wet handkerchief.

They almost reached the door of the card room, easily identified because of the sharp smell of cheroot smoke from within. She had to answer him soon if she had any hope of learning more.

"I'm afraid her sister was a bit vapid. I'm not sure whether to trust what she told us or not."

"Annandale will have it out of Miss Burwick. You might as well tell me."

Sard it! Katherine had left the pair alone because she'd thought they wanted the time. Only with Wayland's words did she recall Pru's warning not to leave her alone with her fiancé, because she feared what she might let slip. Then again, Pru had *arrived* with her fiancée, so if she hadn't already slipped up, then she probably wouldn't do it now. At this point, Katherine only hoped that the avenue of information went both ways.

She arched an eyebrow. "The same might be said for Lord Annandale. Did you find Mr. Blake's information trustworthy?"

Wayland shrugged. The play of his muscles carried down his arm to where her fingers rested on his sleeve. "As trustworthy as a man of his ilk can be."

"What is that supposed to mean?"

"He's a merchant," Wayland answered.

For a moment, Katherine couldn't breathe. She'd

thought Wayland to have as liberal a view on classes as did she. Had she been wrong? But he broke bread with Lyle without complaint, and hadn't seemed to mind including McTavish in his investigation. How could he think himself, the son of a viscount, so above a man who worked for a living like Mr. Blake?

"I beg your pardon?"

Her cutting tone appeared to take him aback. A step away from the door, with the smoke starting to sting her eyes, he halted.

"Lower your hackles, Katherine. I know his type, and it has little to do with his lack of a title. He's a skinflint — out to make money and keep it by any means, legal or not. Always willing to capitalize on another, especially those he employs. He isn't what I would classify as a good man."

Katherine crossed her arms, if only to add a little more distance between them. "How does that differ from most peers?"

"It doesn't," Wayland answered without heat.

Some of the tension leached out of her shoulders with his honesty.

With a shrug, he rubbed the back of his neck before dropping his hand to his side once more. "I'm only telling you my observations. Have you met him?"

She fought the urge to nibble on a fingernail as she

thought. "I can't recall. I might have done, but men without titles in their lineage aren't usually invited to the same gatherings I am, barring the Society of course."

"Of course." He nodded, having attended those same Royal Society for Investigative Techniques meetings.

She brought her hand halfway to her lips before she balled it and fisted it at her side. She admired the garland decorating a painting on the wall, of a summer country landscape. "So you don't trust what he told you about Ellie. Do you think he killed her?"

When she met Wayland's gaze, he raised his eyebrows pointedly. "Do you?"

"I haven't spoken with him yet."

"Yet." A smirk teased at the corner of his mouth as he leaned forward again, playful. "So you do intend to speak with him."

"I never said otherwise. I won't cut out suspects or informants, I simply said that speaking to Ellie's sister *first* would be more expedient." She turned her back on him, effectively ending the conversation before he could make a rebuttal. As she faced the card room, the haze of smoke making the figures inside blur, she caught sight of a portly man of middling height and thick black hair. He looked to be fifty or so, and she recognized him immediately.

"What is Mr. Blake doing here?" Though Katherine had only seen him a few times and fleetingly if that, she had an impressive memory that most people did not share. She frowned, squinting to make certain that she hadn't mistaken him for someone else.

No, certainly that was he. In the style of a lord, he'd taken to crafting himself a crest. His depicted a tall glass of wine in front of a barrel with an ornate ring of laurel leaves around it. He must own a vineyard somewhere, though Katherine had never looked into it. Unlike most peers, who weren't so vain as to blatantly wear the crests of their ancestors, Mr. Blake had had his stitched into the weave of his jacket.

"The hostess must be desperate to invite him to her Christmas ball." It was an observation, not censure. Most peers would have eschewed the idea of meeting Mr. Blake on equal footing, and not only because he bartered goods. The crest on his jacket proclaimed his intentions loud and clear — he undoubtedly wanted a lord for his daughter to marry, and the lords with any sense would prefer not to align themselves with so grasping a man as he, regardless of his money. Those lords without money usually did not have much sense either, having spent it.

"Indeed she must."

Wayland's words were clipped. He had a dangerous air to him, like a tiger coiled to strike. As he clamped his hand around her elbow, she reflexively tried to pull away. He held fast and leaned closer to whisper in her ear.

"Come back to the ballroom. It's safer."

Safer? She bristled. "I beg your pardon? We're at a ball."

"Yes, and the man Mr. Blake is playing cards with has been known to play loosely with the law. Ask your father if you don't believe me."

As he tried to pull her away, Katherine dug in her heels and squinted to see the other man. The angle was poor, and the cheroot dangling from his lips added more smoke to the room. Still, there was something about him she couldn't quite place...

"He looks familiar..."

Wayland adjusted his hand from her elbow to her back. His strength outmatched hers, and she stumbled forward before she fell. He used the momentum to his advantage, walking her past the room and toward the light and music pouring from a doorway at the end of the corridor. That room must connect to the one they had left in the line forming the ballroom.

"He recently inherited his title, which only gave

him more money to use to evade the law. Now please, come quietly."

She did, but she couldn't shake the feeling that something in that card room could have pointed her to Ellie's murderer. As they paused in the doorway, she tilted her head up to read Wayland's expression. "You don't think his association with Mr. Blake has anything to do with the murder, do you?"

Wayland's mouth curved up. He winked at her. "Now, Lady Katherine, why would I tell you my suspicions? I have a wager to win."

She stepped away from him with alacrity. The warmth of his hand dropped away from her back just as she spotted Pru, who seemed to have slipped free of her fiancé. With a bullish expression, Pru stormed up to them and caught Katherine's hand, towing her away. Loudly, she said, "You must come with me to speak to Lady Dalhousie. She told me that Lord Conyers might be selling his townhouse."

"Oh?" Katherine fought the urge to glance over her shoulder at Wayland. As Pru led her between dancing couples to the far side of the ballroom, Katherine felt his gaze on the back of her neck.

When they were far enough away, she whispered, "Brilliant excuse."

Pru paused to link her arm through Katherine's

instead of dragging her along by the hand. All the easier to speak. "It isn't an excuse, not precisely. She did tell that to me, and I promised to fetch you to hear more. I assume you're still interested in the house?"

Only a month ago, Lord Conyers had used a house he'd purchased on St. James's Square to hold sordid trysts. Despite the history of the house, it was conveniently located near to a park for Emma to romp and within walking distance of Pall Mall Street, where the Society held their monthly meetings. It also happened to be nearby to Lord Annandale's townhouse, should Pru and he be in residence. To Katherine, the location was ideal.

But would the price be as ideal? She had to live off of her dowry for the rest of her years. That, or keep herself flush with matchmaking clients. Since she kept her work as a detective a secret to avoid becoming a pariah and reflecting poorly on her family, she was rarely paid for any of her detective work.

"Katherine?"

She offered her friend a smile. "I am, of course."

"Good. Lady Dalhousie is right this way."

The moment a couple danced out of their path, Katherine noticed Lady Dalhousie immediately. She wore a gown of ice blue to complement the waterfall of aquamarines and diamonds ringing her neck. Her gray hair was covered by an elaborate feathered turban, leaving her ears free to sparkle under the weight of more diamonds.

She greeted Katherine warmly as they reached her. Katherine deftly avoided having to kiss the old woman's cheek. They weren't that good of friends. In fact, Katherine had first encountered her because she had lost the very same necklace she now wore while in Bath this past September. Katherine used her for information, nothing more.

"Pru tells me you've heard that Lord Conyers is selling his St. James's townhouse."

"Yes," the old woman agreed, nodding vigorously enough to make her cheeks jiggle. "The one on Charles Street." She lowered her voice to a conspiratorial level. "I hear his fiancée is forcing him to do so, or else she'll call off the engagement. He's quite desperate to be rid of it."

Was he, now? Katherine tucked away a smile. "Perhaps he'd be willing to negotiate on the price, then."

"Oh, I'd say so. His fiancée is a wealthy heiress, he won't be willing to let her slip away, now would he?"

Katherine would rather not discuss Lord Conyers's fickle heart. His predicament with his bride-to-be was precisely why Katherine had never wanted to marry.

Too many gentlemen would see her as nothing more than a fat purse. Add to that the fact that few would accept her chosen career, and her decision to remain unwed and devote herself to her work became the sole sensible choice.

"Speaking of infidelities," Lady Dalhousie said with unbridled glee, "Miss Burwick and I were just discussing Mr. Blake. You know the fellow, he imports goods for half the shops in London? Silly little things mostly, like woven cotton from the Americas."

"He's not faithful to his wife?" Katherine took care to keep her voice low. When she glanced over her shoulder, searching for Wayland, she couldn't find him. She couldn't make up her mind whether that boded good or ill. At the very least, he wouldn't over-hear this particular lead in the investigation.

She had hoped that, through speaking with Lady Dalhousie, she and Pru would discover this very thing. Now the only question was whether Lady Dalhousie could confirm if Ellie Simpson had been his mistress.

"Indeed not, such a shame, it is. I've heard he even beds his own staff, right under his wife's nose! Poor dear. I wouldn't be surprised if the rumors that she, too, looks elsewhere are true. If it were I, I would look within my own household too, just to spite him." Lady Dalhousie clucked her tongue. "I assure you, I never would have stood for such disrespect while my husband was alive. But then, Mrs. Blake cares too much for money, doesn't she? Not that her husband seems to give her much rein. I see the same, sad old jewels on her neck. I hear he won't let her spend a penny on new ones, and I've never known him to give her even one gift. I wonder what gifts he gives his mistresses, don't you?"

Lady Dalhousie tapped her finger against her lips, the barest pause before she launched into the infidelities of other acquaintances in High Society. Katherine listened with only half an ear, far too concerned with the information.

Mr. Blake took his servants to bed.

Ellie Simpson had been one of his servants.

Ellie had had a silver bracelet and lace-edged nightgown.

But, according to Wayland, Mr. Blake kept his money close. Had he been dallying with Ellie before her death? When it came to the gossip that fell from Lady Dalhousie's mouth, Katherine couldn't be too careful. She needed to verify the matter.

She needed to send Harriet into the Blake household, after all. As soon as may be.

CHAPTER FIVE

If a young woman hadn't been killed and left bereft of justice, Harriet Wood would never have volunteered to help anyone do laundry, not even Gabrielle. Her friend, a short, dark woman, stabbed the business end of a stick into the steaming tub of hot water and limp, dirty clothes and swished them around. The hideous odor of lye permeated the windowless room in the ground floor of Mr. Blake's house, stinging Harriet's nose.

Before coming to work for Lady Katherine, Harriet had spent her time washing the soiled underclothes of the wealthy. It was a fetid, thankless job. The lye used to wash the clothes left her hands dry and cracked, undoing the help of Lady Katherine's thoughtful gift. Harriet had thus far used the lotion only sparingly, not wanting to waste it. After today, she might have to coat her hands in the entire jar to feel soft again.

Taking a deep breath, she plunged her hands into the hot water. The water and lye assaulted her skin. The steam wafted into her face, stinging her nostrils and leaving her red-eyed. No, Harriet would prefer to clean chamber pots than do laundry. But Gabrielle's job here was to wash the clothes and linens, so Harriet bit the inside of her cheek and fished around for one of the nightdresses. She scrubbed it vigorously against the washboard and wrung it out, wincing as the water sank into cuts in her hand too small for her eyes to see. As she pulled the dripping garment free, she glanced at her friend.

How could Gabrielle look so composed? She must abhor the wash as much as Harriet, yet her expression was set as she prodded at the nightdress beneath her stick a few more times. Perhaps because she had yet to wet her hands.

Turning over the fine muslin nightdress in her hands, Harriet asked, "Does your mistress embroider her initial into the cloth? I don't want to mix hers with anyone else's in the house."

Lady Katherine had sent her to infiltrate the house and learn what she could, but Harriet didn't know whether she could call herself a detective. She'd decided, before stepping foot into Mr. Blake's domain, that she would approach Gabrielle as a friend.

The fellow maid shook her head, her mouth set in a solemn line. "No. It's only she and little Chastity in the house. Chastity is only fourteen — that, there, is her dress. You'll notice the size difference."

Chastity, the initial C. Given what Lady Katherine had disclosed, the nightgown that Ellie Simpson possessed would not have come from the child. But what about Mrs. Blake?

Harriet hummed tunelessly under her breath as she draped the damp dress over the rungs of the clotheshorse climbing across the ceiling. "I'll never understand why these lofty folks think names like Chastity are good for their daughters. What is her mother named, Purity?"

Her friend laughed and separated a set of stockings from choking a larger nightdress. "Virginia, actually."

If anything, that name was worse. And it began with a V — not an M. Harriet didn't like to give information to Lady Katherine that discounted a possibility, but the nightgown could not have been handed down from one of the two women in the house. Stifling a wash of disappointment, Harriet applied herself to the next item in the wash basin. She answered absently.

"Women are not delicate flowers, no matter what men might want us to be."

Gabrielle snorted. "The women belonging to lords and merchants might as well be. They're brought up to be soft." She leaned down, snagging the much larger nightdress and beating it over the washboard, her face set.

It was true. For all of Lady Katherine's brilliance, Harriet couldn't picture her washing clothes. Still, Gabrielle's comment raised her hackles. The wooden beams of the clotheshorse rattled as Harriet tossed the next item over it to dry.

"Lady Katherine is no delicate flower. She's all mettle." Her inability to wash clothes notwithstanding.

Gabrielle clucked under her tongue as she continued to work. "If she is, it's no thanks to her parents. I've seen the way they, men and women alike, treat their daughters. As if they're too fragile and must be hidden away from the world."

The bitterness in her friend's voice silenced Harriet, even if she didn't entirely agree. She hadn't been with the Dorchester household while Katherine had been young, but from the moment she'd earned her position, the earl had treated his daughter with an unparalleled respect. At first, it had made Harriet rather envious. She hadn't been born into a household that thought women could accomplish less work than men, but she had never been treated in the same way, either. To the Earl of Dorchester, his daughter was his equal.

Arguing about it wouldn't earn her the information she had come to learn, however, so she continued to work alongside Gabrielle in silence. When the sting in her hands became unbearable, Harriet straightened and flexed them at her sides. She wasn't accustomed to so much washing at once anymore. If the house was busy, she sometimes helped with Lady Katherine's things, but not every week.

Idly rubbing at her sore hands, she leaned against the wall for a moment. "I hear Mr. Blake doesn't care to part from his money. Has he replaced the maid who died this summer ... was her name Ellie?"

"Yes, Ellie." Gabrielle sighed, long and hard. "I wish he had replaced her. I'm doing my job *and* hers now because Rita barely lifts a finger if she can help it."

Harriet pursed her lips. "Who is Rita?" Moreover — was she important?

"Another maid in the house." Gabrielle straightened with a groan, rubbing the small of her back with wet hands. "She's meant to keep the house from gathering dust, but I think she spends more time straightening the beds than anything else. She certainly takes her time about them."

The tone of her discontent piqued Harriet's interest, but she bit her tongue. She wasn't here to glean drops of gossip. Her first priority must be learning more about the poor young woman left unavenged.

"I don't know how Ellie put up with her. She and Rita used to split the chores, and they still seemed thick as thieves."

Straightening from the wall, Harriet stopped rubbing at her hands. She studied her friend in the light seeping in from the next room. "If I'm honest, I didn't come here only to help with laundry."

Gabrielle laughed, a mirthless, tired sound. "Why would you? You have a comfortable life with Lady Katherine, I hear."

Was that jealousy? "I do my work."

"I hear the bulk of your duties involve caring for her silly little dog."

The accusation stung. She hadn't gentled into some soft-handed, airheaded lady since taking the position with Lady Katherine. If anything, Harriet had been challenged in ways she hadn't considered before joining Dorchester House. "I do more than that, I assure you. And Emma is sweet! You ought to meet her before you disparage her."

Gabrielle raised her hands, palms out. "Peace. I didn't mean to offend. I'm not likely to chase off the only friend who will help me with the chores."

Perhaps she was being too sensitive. Saying nothing, she tried to accept the apology as they resumed working. It still rankled. Nevertheless, she pressed her lips together and stepped closer to help rinse and hang the rest of the wash.

"Why did you come, if not to help with the laundry?"

Without looking at her friend, Harriet continued with the chores. "What more can you tell me about Ellie?"

The silence stretched on so long, Harriet thought it might snap. When she raised her gaze, she found Gabrielle's eyebrows hooked together in wariness.

Harriet battled away a frown. "Should I not have asked?"

"I'm not the person you ought to ask." Gabrielle's words emerged thick and reluctant, like treacle. "If I'm honest, I knew Ellie very little. I didn't care to know her better, as long as she kept herself out of my way and did her work." Another long, pregnant pause before she added softly, "Why are you asking?"

Harriet didn't know how to answer, so she said

nothing at all, continuing to work as if she hadn't heard.

A ponderous expression crossed her friend's face. "I've heard things about your mistress..."

Harriet would never feed gossip about Lady Katherine. Her voice cutting, she asked, "If not you, then who should I ask?"

Gabrielle took a small step back, her hands clenching around the sopping stockings she held. Water dripped from the fabric onto her shoes, but she didn't appear to notice. She pressed her lips together before answering softly, thoughtfully, "Rita might be best. Like I said, they were friendly and tended to keep company even when not on duty." After a moment's hesitation, Gabrielle added, "I can introduce you."

Harriet nodded. "Please. Let's finish with the wash and do that."

As she pegged more clothes onto the line, the barest whisper of Gabrielle's voice lit the air. Harriet couldn't be certain that she heard correctly, the voice was so soft.

"I've heard things about you, too."

RITA WAS A REMARKABLY COMELY young woman

with porcelain skin, straw-blond hair, and an evasive way of answering even the simplest of questions. Luckily, Harriet had practice in keeping her demeanor friendly despite irritations, what with Lady Katherine keeping company with men like Lord Annandale these days, or, more specifically, his valet, McTavish.

Harriet refused to let anyone, let alone a woman like Rita, stop her from bringing justice to Ellie Simpson. And if she happened to prove to McTavish that she shouldn't be underestimated, all the better.

His blatant disregard for the feminine sex had irked her from the moment they'd met. He saw her — and likely every other female — as nothing more than a product of her gender, there to be pleased and to please him. Well, she had no intention of pleasing him or indulging his flirtations. She didn't know why Lady Katherine hadn't put him in his place a long time ago. But if her employer would not, Harriet would. And she would do it by first getting him to acknowledge that she was his intellectual equal.

Rita hunched her shoulders, thereby stuffing her hands farther into the pocket of the apron at her waist. A bulge drew the eye to the apron, where she likely kept her feather duster.

She met Harriet's question with the briefest narrowing of her eyes before looking away. "I don't know much about Ellie. She was her own person. Why should I care how she spends her free time? Not that we have much of it. *We* have work."

Not according to Gabrielle. Harriet bit her tongue. She took a deep breath to control herself. "I'm told you were close. You must have known something about her."

Rita shrugged. She averted her gaze and tapped her toe, making it perfectly clear that she would prefer to be anywhere but with Harriet. "We work together. We aren't sisters."

Harriet stifled a sigh. If nothing else, this foray provided her with a newfound respect for Lady Katherine and the lengths to which she put herself to bring justice to the dead. "Very well, then what of Mr. Blake? Did he approve of Ellie and her work?"

"Don't trouble yourself with Mr. Blake," Rita snapped.

Her sudden fierce tone took Harriet aback.

"Look to Mrs. Blake. The household is the wife's responsibility, or isn't it the same in yours?"

Harriet took her direction from Lady Katherine and would follow her when she left Dorchester House. She bit back the urge to defend her employer. "What did Mrs. Blake think of Ellie?" She wasn't leaving without an answer.

Rita didn't seem to notice or care for her determination. The blond maid shrugged. "Do I look like a lofty lady? I don't know."

Sarcasm bubbled to the edge of her tongue, but Harriet bit it back. "What can you tell me about the night Ellie died?"

"Nothing."

"Did you see her that night before she went out? Did she tell you where she was going?"

"No. I wasn't here."

Harriet frowned. "You weren't? Where else would you be?"

"I'll have you know that I was on Brixton Hill." At the disbelieving look Harriet pierced her with — she would have had to leave the city proper in order to reach Brixton — Rita stiffened. "Thanks to the Vauxhall Bridge, it's only a short ride away by coach. I go every time I hear of a bad thunderstorm. Ma doesn't take well to thunderstorms, not after what happened to Pa."

Lady Katherine would say that was either too much detail to be a lie, or too much fiction. Harriet couldn't recall which, and Rita's demeanor did little to help her decide whether to believe the woman.

Since she wasn't likely to receive another answer, she moved on. "Very well. You weren't here. What time did you leave? Was Ellie still in the house when you did?"

"I don't remember."

Harriet clenched and unclenched her fists. "Would someone else know?"

Rita shrugged. Even before she opened her mouth, Harriet knew she would get no information out of the intended response.

Frustrated, she cut off the other woman with thick sarcasm. "You don't know."

Control yourself.

She took a steadying breath before she continued in a measured tone. "What can you tell me regarding her relationships with those in the house?"

"Nothing. Like I said, we aren't sisters."

Harriet should have anticipated that answer, but it rattled her composure nevertheless. If she left now, she would have to tell Lady Katherine that she had learned nothing. Moreover, it would give McTavish and his team an advantage if they'd learned something from Mr. Blake. That was unacceptable.

"Did any of the visitors give her particular attention?"

Based on the slash of Rita's mouth, they hadn't.

"The footmen, or even Mr. Blake?"

Rita's expression soured. She turned her face away

and mumbled something that Harriet didn't quite catch.

"What was that? Is it something about the attention she received?"

Rita glared at the floor. "I'm certain she garnered plenty of male attention, since she was so beautiful. I didn't see anyone here with her." Despite her tone, she didn't meet Harriet's gaze directly. Could she simply be protecting her friend's good name?

Her words were clipped, her hands were in her pocket, the bulge jiggling as if she toyed with the feather duster while she spoke, and she refused to look Harriet in the eye. Every line in Rita's body bespoke a nervous, standoffish woman. Not helpful in the least. Should she have tried to woo Rita into becoming her friend? That tack took time. And with the wager between her employer and Captain Wayland, it was time she didn't have to give. Lady Katherine expected information.

Despite Harriet's attempts, Rita had little to give. An evasive woman like Rita wouldn't give her more information. The longer she kept the woman from her work, the more suspicious it would look. In case someone in the household had killed Ellie, Harriet decided to admit defeat gracefully. Trying to hide her dejection, she bid Rita adieu and slipped out of the laundry room. Within minutes, she was wrapped in her cloak and shutting the servants' door behind her.

Although the snow had stopped falling, cold wrapped around her like a shroud. Hard crusts of snow crunched beneath her boot as she began the walk back to Dorchester House. As she slipped between two houses, thinking to cut across the line of tall fences separating the gardens of the wealthy, a familiar voice caught her attention.

"...and who would nae?"

McTavish.

Every muscle in her body hardened. She held herself poised along a fence taller than her head, her breathing shallow as she listened to the exchange. The fence belonged to Mr. Blake's townhouse. McTavish must be on the other side, speaking to someone in the household. Why hadn't she considered that he, too, would insert himself into the house? She'd nearly been caught! She held her breath, not daring to make a sound lest she alert him to her eavesdropping.

"No, I mean he's had lots of women." The voice, also male, was thick with inebriation. Come to think of it, McTavish's voice had been a touch slurred, his brogue thicker than usual. Was he out drinking with one of the footmen? Given the location, they must have raided Mr. Blake's cellar for the drink. She nearly clucked her tongue before she bit it instead.

On the other side of the fence, the footman started naming women. "Chastity's governess, the scullery maid, had an actress for a while, Mr. Roland's wife — he's the fellow next door — that saucy blonde who cleans the bedchambers." He snapped his fingers, an absent and uncoordinated sound as he hummed under his breath.

The smack of the wood near to her head would have made her yelp if she hadn't already been biting her tongue. Her teeth gouged hard into her flesh as she jumped. Wincing, she unclenched her jaw.

"Ouch." The man hissed.

Ouch, indeed.

His voice warm with triumph, McTavish asked, "You would nae mean Ellie Simpson, the woman who died?"

Harriet released her breath as the notion dawned. Had Mr. Blake been taking Ellie to bed? He was rich enough to provide her with the gifts Lady Katherine had learned of. But if he was so cheap as not to replace a valued maid, would he spend money on gifts for her? No, he would be more likely to keep them after their tryst ended.

But the bracelet had not been among the belongings given to Ellie's sister. Perhaps she had been entertaining Mr. Blake privately and he'd taken it back.

The footman *tsked*. "Could be. Rita — Rita is the one I meant. Can't get her to look sideways at a man. At least, not one so low as me."

So Rita was bedding Mr. Blake. No wonder she had acted so odd. Harriet shook her head but breathed shallowly as she listened to the conclusion of the interview. Both men continued to drink, their words slurring more until, disgusted at the lack of further information, she finally left. McTavish was a brute, but at least he was good for something. She stepped lightly, trying not to give away her footsteps as she hurried back to Dorchester House.

Her employer was waiting, and she couldn't wait to share this information. Because of her conversation with Rita, she knew something McTavish did not know. And soon, Lady Katherine would know of it, too.

CHAPTER SIX

Katherine listened attentively as Harriet recounted her morning in detail for the second time. Although her words were delivered without protest, they held a note of exasperation. Katherine tried not to take offense. As much as she trusted Harriet, she needed to make certain that she had the correct facts, and that meant repetition. Once Harriet was done, Katherine sat back on the neatly made four-poster bed that dominated her bedchamber and idly scratched Emma behind the ears.

"You're certain the man McTavish was talking to only mentioned Rita by name?"

"Yes."

Katherine would have preferred more concrete

evidence that Ellie was involved, but this was enough to draw her suspicions.

Lowering herself onto the bed next to Katherine, Pru said, "But the man did say that Mr. Blake was bedding other maids in the house, didn't he?"

Again, Harriet nodded. "Yes. I didn't talk to him myself or I would have confirmed Ellie in particular."

Katherine frowned. "McTavish did not?"

"He didn't."

How curious. Katherine had to assume that McTavish was being instructed in the techniques of investigation by Wayland in the same way that he had taken Lord Annandale under his wing. She knew better than to underestimate Wayland. He was an accomplished detective, and he would have stressed the need to verify information. Perhaps this man wasn't the only one with whom McTavish had spoken.

The other two women in the room had already moved on from the peculiarity of McTavish's sloppy investigating. Pru leaned forward on the edge of the bed, her eyes locked with Harriet's as she peppered the standing woman with questions.

"Do you think Mr. Blake killed Ellie?"

"Why would he?"

"An excellent question, Harriet," Katherine interjected. She held up her finger, regaining control of the conversation. "Let's assume that Ellie was in fact having an affair with Mr. Blake. For him to buy her gifts and give her the use of his carriage, he must have liked her."

Harriet frowned. "He let her use the carriage? No one told me that."

Had Katherine left that out when she'd recounted the facts?

Pru answered as Katherine frowned, too engrossed in recalling her previous conversation. She should have been more attentive than that. As a member of the team, Harriet needed to know everything they did.

"Her sister told us that she saw Ellie in town one day getting into a carriage with Mr. Blake's crest on it."

Harriet frowned, deep grooves of suspicion forming around her mouth and nose. She said nothing — nothing needed to be said.

"The carriage is one thing. It costs Mr. Blake nothing to let her use it. Or rather, nothing but an inconvenience should it be out when he wants it." Katherine chewed on her thumbnail as she thought. "When I was at the ball yesterday, Wayland called him a skinflint. But he certainly doesn't fit that description if he's going around buying gifts for his mistresses."

Pru raised her eyebrows. "Do you think Wayland was lying to you to lead your investigation astray?"

"Do you?"

The idea sat ill in Katherine's stomach. Logically, she knew she couldn't trust Wayland. Her father was a supreme judge of character, and even if Wayland had been nothing but helpful to her investigations thus far, he had to have some motive to help that Katherine had not yet ascertained. But the idea that he would deliberately try to lead her astray when a woman's life had been lost made her stomach curdle. He wasn't that sort of man ... was he? Her instincts warred with logic.

Seeming to sense her unease, Pru reached out and squeezed Katherine's knee. "I don't. And besides, Lady Dalhousie also said Mr. Blake was cheap. But if you're afraid he did, I'll ask my Annandale."

A small smile tugged at the corners of Katherine's mouth. Pru refused to use her husband's given name aloud, claiming it was hers to use. Now that she'd settled on a match, she seemed remarkably territorial. "*My* Annandale" was new.

Harriet interrupted before Katherine answered. "Captain Wayland did not lie. Mr. Blake is certainly a skinflint."

Katherine raised her gaze to her friend in askance. "What makes you think he is so trustworthy?"

Harriet crossed her arms over her chest. She wore one of Katherine's cast-offs, a dowdy color and cut that Katherine was just now realizing looked horrid, even if she dressed that way on purpose to disabuse men from the notion of courting her. But Harriet shouldn't suffer for her decisions. Perhaps she ought to find a reason to pass along a few of her other colorful dresses.

"I'm not contesting his trustworthiness, though he seems a perfectly fine gentleman to me." At Katherine's glare she added, "This wager aside. No, I'm saying that the information is correct. Despite losing a maid this summer, Mr. Blake has yet to replace her. My friend is doing Ellie's work as well as her own. It isn't fair to the household."

Solemnly, Katherine nodded to indicate her agreement. "Then Mr. Blake isn't one to spend money."

"If he had, perhaps someone got jealous that they weren't given a bracelet too," Pru suggested. "The footman mentioned Rita in particular. Perhaps she killed Ellie."

Harriet hummed under her breath. "She told me she was out of the city that night, but I find it a flimsy excuse. She was acting odd, and that might have been why."

Although Katherine trusted her friend's assessment, she added, "It could be Mrs. Blake, too. If her husband was so cheap that he never bought her jewelry — and Lady Dalhousie told us that Mrs. Blake enjoys having money at her fingertips — then what would she do if she learned that he'd given Ellie a bracelet and expensive clothes?"

Finishing Katherine's thought, Pru answered, "If I was her, I wouldn't like it one bit. But she couldn't have known about the nightgown."

Katherine suggested, "Perhaps she saw Ellie wearing the bracelet."

"Where is this bracelet?" Harriet asked. "I still haven't seen it."

"Neither have I."

Pru tapped her toe on the floor, a sharp rhythm. "Do you think the killer took it? I do think this death is more than a simple theft, but it might have been revenge and theft, too."

Katherine looked at her maid. "Was Rita wearing jewelry today?"

Harriet nibbled on her lower lip. "I don't know. She had her hands in her pockets the entire time we spoke. I didn't think much of it, since she seemed rather nervous, but I would have paid more attention had I known."

"So she could have been wearing the bracelet right there in front of you."

Harriet hesitated before she shook her head. "I don't think so. Why would you wear jewelry to work? Anyone who came into the house might assume that you are stealing from your betters. No, if Rita does have it, I imagine she has it hidden away somewhere."

Katherine nodded. "*If* Rita killed Ellie. If Ellie's killer was Mrs. Blake..."

Thoroughly ignored and feeling sore about it, Emma attacked Katherine's hand, nudging it with her nose in a demand to be petted. Katherine tipped the pug onto her back on the pink coverlet and rubbed her belly, but the attack gave her an idea.

"If Mrs. Blake has so little jewelry, she will surely wear the same pieces over and over again. A new bracelet to add into the mix would be something to show off."

Pru met her gaze, a light shining in her eyes. "You're right. We need to take a look at Mrs. Blake's wrist." She leaned forward, grasping at Katherine's hand and squeezing tight. "Everyone important will be at the theater tonight for the Christmas pantomime. All we need to do is make certain we attend." She released Katherine and pierced her with a coy glance. "I know who will be my escort. And yours, Katherine?"

Katherine groaned. "I don't need an escort."

She glanced at Harriet for help, but her maid suddenly found something to tidy in the nearly spotless room.

"Yes, you do," Pru insisted. "If you don't have an escort, everyone will remark on it."

"Do you think I care if I'm the subject of gossip?"

"Of course not. But you are in the middle of an investigation, and that means not drawing attention to yourself." She fluttered her hand, the one glittering with the ring Lord Annandale had given her, in front of her face. "Perhaps I'll ask my fiancé if he has a friend to accompany you."

Katherine knew precisely who this friend would be. "I would rather send Harriet in my place than go to the theater with Wayland."

Harriet sniggered, but when Katherine looked at her, she was rifling through the desk drawers of the writing desk, straightening the papers.

Pru poked Katherine in the shoulder. "You don't have a choice. It's Christmas, and I want to spend time with my fiancé. That means you'll have to entertain Captain Wayland."

Katherine bit the inside of her cheek and counted to five.

While she was composing herself, Pru drove the

final nail into the coffin. "*If* you care to pursue this investigation."

"Fine," Katherine snapped, though she dearly wished she could ask Lyle to accompany her instead. But he tended to turn as stiff as a board in social situations, where he often told her he had no business being. With a sigh, Katherine capitulated, hoping her family would be too occupied to uncover whom she spent her time with.

"I'll go to the theater with Wayland on one condition: no one must tell him why we're there. I intend to solve this investigation first."

Pru's eyes twinkled as she grinned. "Don't worry. So do I."

CHAPTER SEVEN

The actors of the pantos enthralled the crowd in the tale called *The Harlequin and the Cinderella*. The audience, attention rapt on the stage, decried the heroine's stern father as he tried to force her into a marriage she didn't want. Moments later, her fairy godmother appeared and transformed her into Columbine, a harlequin character complete with a vibrant dress with voluminous skirts reminiscent of a century past. The resultant chase scene that ensued involved acrobatics and flashes of other bright costumes as harlequins and clowns danced around Columbine on stage.

If Katherine hadn't spotted Mrs. Blake near the front of the audience, close to the stage, she would never have chosen so close a position to stand. She adored pantomime, but she wasn't here for the performance. She had a murder to solve and couldn't afford to find herself distracted.

The man on her left was distraction enough. Wayland looked every inch the gentleman tonight in black evening attire. From the moment she and Pru had arrived at the theater, he and Lord Annandale had stuck to them like burrs. Albeit, Pru didn't seem to mind occupying her fiancé in the seats Katherine had eschewed. Unfortunately, Wayland refused to leave her by the aisle.

How was Katherine expected to examine Mrs. Blake's wrists without Wayland discovering what she was on about? She didn't know whether or not he suspected Mrs. Blake for the murder, but if he hadn't considered her yet, Katherine didn't want to tip her hand.

The pantomime figures vaulted off the stage, entering the crowd as they pursued Columbine. The clowns performed complicated acrobatics as she twisted and turned between the members of the audience, whose chairs were positioned far enough apart to allow for this sort of expected audience interaction. Katherine might have been perfectly content to watch the harried scene unfold, the audience members positioning themselves in front of Columbine's pursuers to block them and aid her plight, if she hadn't stumbled directly up to Katherine.

With her pale painted face and exaggerated features, she closed her hands around Katherine's wrists and beseeched her in a staged voice. "Please, madam, you must hide me! If my father discovers me, he'll force me to marry a man I do not want."

Katherine froze. As the daughter of an earl, she garnered some attention from those looking to curry favors with the rich, but she hated being the focus of anything. This was why she never sat close enough to the stage for the pantomime's characters to single her out.

Heart hammering, Katherine took a hasty step back, then another. "Of course," she answered in little more than a mumble. She searched for an escape and found it in Wayland's tall, broad-shouldered form. "Hide here." She thrust the actress behind Wayland's back. The moment the woman released her, Katherine skirted the audience to a safer position closer to the rear door. Wayland was left comically in the middle of the production until Columbine decided that it was safe enough for her to return to the stage.

"I understand how she feels," murmured a woman's voice. Until that moment, Katherine hadn't realized that she had stopped alongside someone she knew. A dark-haired woman's figure unfolded from the aisle seat next to Lord and Lady Brackley. Neither appeared to notice her, so Katherine stepped back to allow Miss Graylocke to rise.

She followed Katherine to the wainscoted wall, where they were alone. No one appeared to be giving them much mind, as intent as they were on the production. For a moment, Katherine thought she noticed a familiar face. Mrs. Fairchild narrowed her eyes at Katherine with a knowing look on her face.

Tarnation! I am not matchmaking Miss Graylocke. Not that the rival matchmaker ever cared to hear the truth. If she wanted to concoct the fiction that Katherine was out to steal her clients, there was nothing Katherine could do to dissuade her.

She turned to Miss Graylocke, who watched her intently as though awaiting a response. "What do you mean?"

Miss Graylocke scanned the crowd, but finding them with their full attention on the performance, she leaned closer and whispered, "I, too, am being forced into a marriage I don't want."

Katherine raised her eyebrows. That was surprising, considering the notoriety of the Graylocke marriages. All five siblings had married for love. Didn't they want the same for their cousin?

Before Katherine probed further, Miss Graylocke surged on. She clasped Katherine's elbow, her grip as tight as a manacle. "I've heard of your reputation as a matchmaker. Is it true?"

Katherine fought back a grimace. Most of the time, her matchmaking work was an essential front for her true passion. It was only in this case that she'd been approached about the murder and not matchmaking.

"That depends on what you've heard."

Miss Graylocke seemed to take that as a confirmation, because she whispered, "Are you able to get somebody *out* of the match? I..."

The young woman sighed, a lock of her black hair falling forward onto her cheek as she turned to peer across the audience. Katherine followed her gaze to a trim young man with reddish hair standing along the wall. Dimly, she recognized him, certain that they had been introduced at some point.

"My parents want me to marry the Duke of Quinbury. But... I can't. I'm in love with Lord Glandore. I'm certain he loves me, too. Could you do something, *anything* to help?"

The last thing Katherine wanted was to find herself playing matchmaker. But the love-struck look on Miss Graylocke's face twisted her heart. Darn it! Perhaps if Lord Glandore had been indifferent, but as she glanced at him once more she found him looking at them with an expression that was nothing short of longing. Katherine never drew that sort of attention, so the look could only be for Miss Graylocke. The two clearly loved each other. Katherine wouldn't be able to live with herself if she didn't help out.

Besides, she'd met the Duke of Quinbury. The pompous arse had all but patted her on the head and praised Papa for putting up with her hanging at his elbow all the time. Katherine had been seventeen.

"Give me a few days. I'll think of something."

The bald relief on Miss Graylocke's face was a reward in itself.

She couldn't afford to find herself peppered with matchmaking questions for the rest of the evening, so she gently excused herself and tiptoed closer to her target. Columbine had returned to the stage, where she was now in the midst of falling in love with Harlequin. Katherine sidled closer to Wayland, who stood between her and Mrs. Blake.

Unfortunately, she still had the problem of deciding how best to distract him.

She stepped to his far side, closer to Mrs. Blake in case she happened to find a reason to approach her target. Wayland raised his eyebrow and gestured at the row of crimson-backed seats. "Should we return to our friends?"

Katherine batted her hand at him. "You go on. I prefer to remain standing."

"In case you need to make a hasty escape?"

He raised his eyebrows and glanced knowingly at the stage. Katherine pressed her lips together, but she couldn't repress a smile.

"Perhaps. I'm sure you don't like being put on the spot any more than I do."

Wayland shrugged. "I've been in worse situations."

He said it with nonchalance, but Katherine knew his demeanor hid something far deeper. When they had visited Bath — not together, but coincidentally at the same time — Captain Wayland had confessed the difficulty of adjusting to civilian life. Granted, he had given her that glimpse because of a mutual friend who had also seen war. His casual comment irked her. She stared at the stage, pretending to be engrossed in the performance.

Unfortunately, he didn't return to his seat. Her father might hate him for whatever reason, but it certainly couldn't be because of Wayland's manners. He was too polite to leave her unescorted ... or perhaps too curious as to why she kept staring at Mrs. Blake. Unbidden, her gaze drifted back to her target. She squinted, trying to discern whether or not the woman wore any jewelry on her wrists. The candlelight in the theater glinted off something metallic, but Katherine couldn't make out any details, not even color. Too many people sat between her and Mrs. Blake.

Katherine took a short step forward, edging her way around the smattering of other people standing in the theater. She glanced over her shoulder, but Wayland didn't seem to notice. She took another short step, then paused. Would she have to wait for intermission?

Another active scene, as Columbine's fairy godmother transformed her for the upcoming ball, erupted onto the stage. Men and women in bright costumes gathered around her, dancing as they trailed ribbons that winked in the candlelight. As the music reached a crescendo, the actors scattered, melting into the crowd to bestow their magic on the audience.

It was precisely the distraction that Katherine needed. As a woman in a garishly bright dress made a beeline for her — had she worn a target on her dress without realizing? — Katherine hurried to evade her, moving closer to Mrs. Blake. The woman must have been blind to Katherine's reluctance. She pursued, brandishing a ribbon. As Katherine tripped on the sloping floor, she staggered closer to Mrs. Blake. With the actress breathing down her neck, she was tempted to flee in earnest. Instead, she used the momentum to fall directly into Mrs. Blake's rotund lap.

If Katherine had fallen into a man's lap, the gossips would have wagged their tongues for weeks. But, considering that she seemed to have earned herself a reputation for clumsiness, she doubted anyone would think twice. As she apologized profusely to Mrs. Blake, she groped for the woman's wrist in search of the bracelet.

She caught only a glimpse of gold before the woman tucked it beneath her opposite hand, hiding it. "Get off! Get off at once!"

Katherine complied. "I'm terribly sorry for the inconvenience."

"We're missing the show!"

Next to her, a young woman no older than fourteen and resembling Mrs. Blake to such a degree that she could only be her daughter, offered Katherine a wan smile. "Are you hurt?"

"No, unsettled is all." A quick glance proved that the actress had moved on to another member of the audience. Mrs. Blake continued to cover her wrists. Katherine would get no further answers.

Had the bracelet been gold just now? Yes, of course. As a child, Katherine had played games with her father to train her mind to notice details like that. If she'd seen gold for a moment, there was no doubt in her mind that Mrs. Blake was not wearing the silver bracelet.

"Perhaps I ought to get you a glass of something fortifying and a seat nearer the back."

Katherine took a step back and collided with Wayland's frame. His expression held as much amusement as his warm tone.

"If you'll excuse us, ladies."

Settling his hand around her elbow, he steered her toward the edge of the audience. Katherine barely noticed his touch, she was so focused on Mrs. Blake.

The bracelet had not matched Sarah Simpson's description. But if the bauble hadn't been stolen, why had Mrs. Blake hidden it? If Mr. Blake was so reluctant about buying jewelry, could she have gotten it by ill means? Perhaps that was why she wanted no one to see it. Perhaps... Perhaps she had traded or pawned the bracelet Ellie Simpson had worn. If she had pawned it, Lyle would know where to look.

Engrossed in her thoughts, Katherine jumped when Wayland leaned closer to whisper in her ear.

"I see you're clumsy tonight."

His voice was low and thick with amusement. He'd been present when she first earned the reputation for being clumsy. He knew that she only used it to investigate. She was not, as a rule, a clumsy person.

"Are you going to tell me what has you looking like a cat about to pounce on a mouse?"

Katherine opened her mouth to give him a smart retort, but Pru and Lord Annandale must have also seen her fall into Mrs. Blake's lap. While the audience had returned their gazes to the events unfolding on stage, the pair sidled through the crowd to meet with Katherine and Wayland at its edge. Both large people, they drew unwanted attention that nearly turned to jeers before startled onlookers recalled Wayland's title.

Pru led the way with eyes that gleamed. She had known of Katherine's intentions this evening. In answer to the unspoken question in her eyes, Katherine shook her head. She couldn't explain her findings until they were alone.

The expectant look on Pru's face fell. Worrying her lower lip, she glanced toward her fiancé and mouthed, "He found something."

Wayland and Annandale, too busy giving each other businesslike nods and steering everyone farther out of the audience's attention, didn't appear to notice. Katherine took advantage of the moment to lean closer to her friend and whisper, "What?"

"I don't know." Pru made a face. She lowered her voice to the barest whisper. "He won't tell me."

Oh, he wouldn't? Katherine loved a challenge. What Lord Annandale knew, Wayland was certain to know as well. As he steered them into the doorway to the lobby, decorated in shades of gold and Christmas boughs, Katherine turned to him with a smirk. She dug in her heels, deeming them far enough away from the performance to speak easily.

"So, how are you enjoying teaching investigation to Lord Annandale?"

Wayland's smile was open, warm, and utterly unexpected given the challenge in her voice. He looked genuinely pleased to be mentoring someone. "You might be surprised how quickly he is catching on. He's showing a lot of promise. Someday he might even out-perform you."

Pru harrumphed. "I'm sure he is. My Annandale is far from dimwitted. But that doesn't mean you lot will be able to unearth the killer before we do."

Katherine grinned. "If Lord Annandale is so astute an investigator, what clues has he found?"

Annandale opened his mouth, but Wayland cut him off with a curt shake of his head. He raised his eyebrows at Katherine. "What clues have you found?"

Katherine scowled. "Nice try, but we aren't telling unless you do."

A pondering expression crossed Wayland's face. "We're in this for the same end. It might do for us to work together if we find ourselves in a bind. I'll admit, we don't have anything concrete at the moment. Do you?"

Reluctantly, Katherine shook her head.

Wayland nodded. "Then let's meet and discuss the clues we found for the sake of catching a killer. Shall we say Monday?"

Katherine shook her head. "I have a family engagement."

"Tuesday, then. In the evening?"

Katherine glanced at Pru to make sure that time was good for her. When she nodded, Katherine turned to Wayland. "You're right. We shouldn't let this killer remain at large for any longer than we need to. Tuesday evening is good for me."

He tipped his head toward her, a smirk curving his lips. "I look forward to hearing whether or not you've gotten any further in your investigation."

It sounded like a challenge. Raising her eyebrows, Katherine assured him, "Oh, I will."

CHAPTER EIGHT

Katherine tucked her red cloak around her shoulders, mirroring the busy mien her friend exuded as they readied themselves to leave Dorchester House. As Pru slipped her hands into her gloves, she glanced over her shoulder at a thundering racket coming down the steps. A moment later, Harriet lurched into view, out of breath, her skirts hiked to her knees. She slid to a stop on the runner in front of Katherine. It bunched beneath her shoes.

"Was that Lyle I saw walking up to the house?"

Katherine frowned. "I really can't—"

The sonorous ring of the brass knocker rippled from the door mere feet away. Rather than wait for the butler, Katherine opened it herself to find Lyle standing on the step. Snowflakes dotted his reddish hair and the shoulders of his greatcoat. When he saw not one but three pairs of female eyes on him, he froze on the step.

Harriet exclaimed, "It *is* him!"

He took a wary step back, scrambling to put his foot on the ground without falling into the banks of snow to either side. "Am I late?"

Katherine had written to him yesterday asking him to look into the various pawn shops in London and discover where they might search to find Ellie Simpson's missing bracelet. Considering how busy he was at work, she had expected him to send back a perfunctory list of establishments rather than offering to escort them himself. However, she was always glad to have his insight along the way. Perhaps more than she cared to admit — his refusal to join her team had hurt.

"You're going out to investigate, aren't you?" Harriet stepped between Katherine and the door, presenting Lyle with her back. Her face was set with determination, her eyes narrowed. "You invited me into this investigation. I'm coming with you."

Katherine had no right to deny her, even if she had to battle with the urge to ask if Harriet had finished her chores for the day.

"We are going to investigate. It may or may not bear fruit. I'm hoping to find Ellie's bracelet at one of the pawn shops. If so, perhaps the proprietor will be able to tell us who sold it to him. We meet with Wayland tomorrow evening."

Harriet crossed her arms over her chest but didn't budge. "I know you do. And I know you're desperate to find evidence that will send the killer to prison."

Katherine made a face. "I'm not desperate. I'm determined."

"We have to win the bet," Pru added. If anything, *she* sounded desperate. What had she wagered with Annandale?

"I know that," Harriet answered, sparing her a mere glance. "But I'm a part of this, too."

Kat interjected, "This bet is about more than our clothing options at the Twelfth Night ball. It's a matter of pride. It's showing the men that women can be just as good if not better than them at investigating."

Behind Harriet, Lyle coughed. With their differences in height, his head showed clear above hers. "Didn't you ask me to join your group?"

Katherine glared at him. He wasn't helping to make her point. "At first. I changed my mind. You're doing quite well in your chosen role of neutral party."

Lyle lifted his hands, palms outward. A sliver of skin showed between the bottom of his leather gloves and the cuff of his greatcoat. "Are we leaving, or will we argue about this more? Because if we're apt to argue, it's frigid out here and I'd like to come inside. Harriet, how can you stand it? You aren't even wearing a jacket."

As dearly as Katherine wanted to bustle them all out of the house and get closer to solving this murder, she stepped to the side to invite him in. Begrudgingly, Harriet shuffled forward, still squarely between Katherine and the door. She glared at Lyle as though it were his fault for interrupting.

"I want to come," she insisted. Perhaps she thought Lyle the weakest link, because she stared him in the eye as she spoke. He turned nearly as red as his hair and stepped back until his back pressed against the door. His posture one of surrender, he beseeched Katherine wordlessly.

Answer her.

Katherine did. "If you're so determined, you may join us."

A smile broke across Harriet's face. She beamed as she took eager steps out of Katherine's path. "I'll wear my new dress. Wait here, I won't be but a moment." And with the clatter of her shoes on the stairs, she bolted up to her quarters. Before she disappeared from view at the landing, she leaned down and pierced Lyle with another glare. "Don't you dare step foot out of this house without me."

He gaped, clearly afraid to say a word. When she disappeared, he turned his gaze on Katherine. "Who stuck the bee in her bonnet?"

Katherine laughed. "I guess she feels more strongly about this investigation than I thought." Considering the stakes, Harriet's enthusiasm could only be an asset.

"This is it," Lyle announced as they stopped in front of an utterly forgettable storefront. Crumbling stucco bracketed the door. No windows faced onto the street. The only indication the edifice served as a shop at all was the teetering sign above the door. Katherine squinted, but the sign was too weathered to make out any words.

"It is?"

Lyle gave her a speaking look. "I know all the pawn shops in London. We've been to the other four. This will be the last."

Under her breath, Pru grumbled, "I sincerely hope

we'll find something here." They hadn't in any of the other shops.

Katherine was disappointed that it had taken so long. She still wanted to question the shop owners in the area where Ellie's body had been found, but the pawn shops had taken up the whole day and all for nothing. Still, she had known there was no guarantee they would find any clues today. Perhaps she was a little desperate, as Harriet had suggested. She wanted something to lord over Wayland at their meeting tomorrow, but thus far all they'd found was tarnished jewelry, faded china, chipped snuff boxes, and various other items that showed their years. No silver-and-ruby bracelets, and none of the shopkeepers had recognized the description.

Wearily, she nodded to indicate the doorway. "Let's go in, then."

As Lyle opened the door for her, she paused. He was so certain this was the last of the pawn shops in London, and he had refused to be on her investigating team... Her gloves squeaked as she clenched her hands.

"Did you know to find this shop because of your work on Bow Street... or because you've already taken Annandale and Wayland here?" If Wayland had gotten here ahead of her... She clenched her fists tighter. The idea rankled.

No, they couldn't have. After all, they didn't know about the bracelet — only she, Pru, and Harriet knew of that. And Lyle, of course.

Lyle fiddled with his collar and said, "I can't tell you anything about Wayland and Lord Annandale's investigation. I have to play fair — I'm not a part of either team."

Scowling, Katherine stepped past him to enter the shop. He stopped her in the threshold with a hand on her arm.

In a low voice, he confessed, "I will tell you they are not any closer to finding the killer than you are. They're following different clues."

So he hadn't shown them the pawn shops. Perversely, that filled her with hope even though they hadn't found a single clue inside the last four they'd inspected. Meeting Lyle's eyes for a moment more, she nodded.

"Thank you."

Upon entering the shop, the four split up to search the wares. Pru hastened to the farthest corner. Harriet lingered near the front while Katherine accompanied Lyle to speak with the shopkeeper.

"Excuse me, sir," he asked, flagging down the thin man with wiry hair to match his spectacles.

"Can I help you?"

Katherine smiled as the man turned to her but didn't introduce himself. The first two shopkeepers hadn't been open to dealing with a woman. Their refusal to speak to her enraged her, but today, finding the bracelet — and thus a clue — was more important than insisting upon equal treatment. As for the latter, she would prove to Wayland that she was the more skilled detective.

Lyle said, "We're looking for a particular piece, if you have it. A family heirloom, but my cousin has gone off and sold it. We're not certain where."

As Lyle had explained, most of the pawn shop owners didn't care to find themselves in the midst of investigations. Too often, they asked no questions of the wares men tried to sell them and unwittingly became fences for stolen goods. Therefore, if they wanted information, the best method was subterfuge.

The man grunted and gestured to his wares. "Feel free to have a look."

"It might have been sold," Katherine interjected. "I'll look, of course, but perhaps you'll recognize it by the description? It's a silver bracelet that clasps together into a heart. In the middle of the heart is a ruby."

The man adjusted his spectacles as he thought, then shook his head. "No, I don't recall a piece like that. But my memory fails me now and then. Feel free to have a look at what's for sale."

Katherine had been given a similar answer at every shop they'd visited thus far. None of them had turned up the bracelet, and she doubted this would, either. Dejected, she rested her hand on a velvet-covered display and stared unblinking at the silver spoons and forks neatly arranged on it. They were a bit tarnished, but the very tips of each flared out into a crest that niggled at the back of her mind. In the same way that her father had trained her to recall crime scenes in great detail, her stepmother had trained her to recognize the crests of the noble houses. Her impeccable memory had come in handy for the dry material.

Why would the Duke of Quinbury's family silver be on this display?

"Katherine?"

"It's nothing," she said absently to Lyle.

Harriet sidled up next to her and peered at the display. "Based on the look on your face, it isn't nothing. What are you looking at?"

"The bracelet couldn't have been melted down so quickly," Lyle informed them. "Even if it had, I doubt that it would have enough material to make even one spoon, let alone all of these."

Katherine shook her head. "No, this is Lord Quinbury's silver. Why would he pawn it?"

"You think he's having money troubles?" Harriet asked.

"It's possible." If so, perhaps she could use that unfortunate fact to dissuade Miss Graylocke's parents from forcing the match. She *had* promised to think on the matter, after all.

She glanced sideways at Harriet. "Do you know anyone in the Quinbury household? Could you ask about his financial situation?" It wasn't uncommon for an old title to have little more than their estate and a mountain of debt. If more titled men and women were keen, like Katherine, to find a means of supporting themselves rather than hemorrhaging money in horse races and gambling dens, perhaps her world would be far different. But with men like Lord Quinbury, appearances were everything. A duke would continue to spend money lavishly even if he had no more to give.

Solemnly, Harriet nodded, but she seemed hesitant. "Do you think this has something to do with the murder?",

"Likely not, but his name has been mentioned in my presence recently, and this seems like an interesting coincidence. I'd like to get to the bottom of it."

She owed a relative of Lady Brackley and Philomena's that much.

LYLE TURNED as pink as Katherine's bedspread whenever he was brought into her bedchambers to discuss a case, so she checked the house before choosing one of the isolated sitting rooms. They needed privacy if they were to discuss the case openly. Once everyone was settled, Harriet included, with a slab of leftover plum pudding and a cup of cider, they went over the clues once more. Katherine held up her finger, pinning Lyle with a stern look.

"None of this is to pass your lips in front of Wayland."

He straightened, tugging on his cuffs. "I have more integrity than that, Katherine. Give me some credit. Let's hear what you have, and I'll give my input if I can."

His offer warmed her. She had been wondering if perhaps he'd come to favor Wayland over her, but it seemed that he truly wished to be a neutral party. She missed investigating with him, to be honest. With a nod, she looked around the room.

In this room, the Christmas decorations were

sparse, only a bit of evergreen trimming the window. The chairs were mismatched and clustered close together around the sole table. The mantel held half-full decanters of brandy, whiskey, and port. The one saving grace of this room was that Emma was permitted to sit on the furniture. She rolled on the cushion next to Harriet, shedding golden hair as she tried in vain to detach the ruby bow around her neck.

"Let's go over the clues, shall we?" When no one protested, she started ticking off items on her fingers. "Ellie was given expensive gifts — the bracelet and her nightgown." Another finger. "Mr. Blake has certainly had affairs with many of the women in his household, but we haven't been able to prove that Ellie was among them."

Harriet shrugged. She looked helpless. "I'm sorry. I tried my best."

Katherine gave her a fond smile. "You have nothing to apologize for. Your efforts have been tremendous so far. It's not always easy to find the information we need." She moved on, holding up another finger. "Mrs. Blake hid the bracelet on her wrist last night, but it was not the one that was given to Ellie. Finally"—she held up another finger—"there is an inconsistency here from what we've learned. Papa instructed me that inconsistencies are never to be overlooked. They are often meaningful to the case. So, we must examine this one. We've been assuming that Ellie was dallying with Mr. Blake and he was giving her gifts. However, all authorities indicate that he hoards his money. He doesn't give gifts to his wife, so why would he give one to a lowly housemaid?"

Harriet drew herself up. "I beg your pardon!"

Katherine winced. "Forgive me, I meant no offense. I meant only to illustrate his mindset, not mine."

Fortunately, Pru steered the conversation back to the matter at hand and saved her from the awkward moment. "Do you think Ellie was special to him in some way?"

"Leopards don't change their spots," Lyle answered. "It could be that Mr. Blake was not the one who gave gifts to the victim. It could have been someone else..." When everyone's eyes turned toward him, he blushed and shrugged his shoulders. He looked at no one in particular when he added, "A maid who dallies with one person may dally with many."

Harriet, the closest to him, smacked him soundly on the arm. "That isn't true at all. Simply because a woman decides to keep company with a man does not mean she decides to keep company with *every* man. Her lot in life has nothing to do with it."

At that, Katherine had to nod.

Lyle shuffled sideways, putting himself out of reach. "I didn't say you did the same. Why would I? You're—" He made a peculiar choking sound and cleared his throat, turning fuchsia.

Good choice. He'd only been digging himself a deeper hole.

When he had himself under control, he continued without looking Harriet in the eye. "I'm speaking hypothetically. If the victim happened to entertain more than one gentleman, one of those men might have killed her out of jealousy. Especially if she spurned his advances later on because she liked another person better."

Harriet glowered at him but didn't make another protest.

Pru tapped her toe audibly. "But who would it be? We haven't been able to find anyone who can say that she's kept company with any man."

Katherine nodded. "And this still doesn't discount Mr. Blake. After all, she was riding in his carriage. But now, we need to figure out if she had any other men in her life." She lifted her gaze to Harriet's and raised her eyebrows.

Harriet sighed. "I'll return to the Blake household and speak with my friend again. She'll put me to work." She lowered her voice to such a grumble that Katherine almost didn't hear.

Since Harriet didn't sound as though she intended the room to hear, Katherine added, "This other maid you spoke with, Rita, she was certainly going to bed with Mr. Blake. Therefore, anything she told you about Ellie must be taken with a grain of salt. I hope your other friend will have more reliable gossip."

Harriet nodded, though she seemed reluctant. "She will. I've never known her to lie to me."

"Good." Katherine turned to Lyle. "Ellie's sister had her things in a box. One item was a beaded reticule. It was water stained, and she said Ellie had had it with her the night she was killed."

Lyle pressed his lips together as if thinking. "Yes, I remember that being one of the items on the list."

"She said it was empty."

Lyle nodded. "That's correct."

Pru made a face. "Why would someone carry an empty reticule?"

Lyle raised a brow. "I asked that myself. One conclusion. She used all her money to purchase something before she died."

Katherine thought about the items in the box. There had been no new purchases. "Was that purchase found with her?"

Lyle frowned. "No. She simply had her clothing and the purse."

"It appears she was missing more than just the bracelet, then," Pru said.

"All the more reason for us to go to the area she was murdered and ask around," Katherine said.

"If we can just find time. The holiday festivities are putting a damper on our investigation." Pru clucked under her tongue and helped herself to more of her plum pudding. Shaking her head as she tucked the morsel in her mouth, she swallowed before saying, "And you'd think all this talk of cheating husbands would put me off marriage for good."

Alarm trailed down Katherine's spine. She wasn't thinking of calling off the wedding, was she? She and Lord Annandale adored each other.

"Has it?"

Pru beamed. "Not at all. In fact, I'm more eager than ever to get married. I think I might have to set a date. After this investigation is over, of course."

Katherine smiled, but it was bittersweet. "That sounds like a splendid idea." She was happy — more than happy for her friend. But she did wish that Lord Annandale didn't live quite so far away. Whatever the case, she would move on with her life, but she would miss her friend.

At least she would still have Lyle and Harriet.

Emma jostled her leg, and Katherine glanced down into the pug's wide-eyed face. Her smile turned genuine as she scratched her dog behind the ears. *And Emma.* She would always have Emma, too.

CHAPTER NINE

Harriet was a bit skeptical about what Lord Quinbury had to do with the investigation at hand. According to Lady Katherine's comment, he didn't, but Katherine still wished for the information, and if Katherine wanted her to glean information, that was what she would do. Unfortunately, her investigation of Lord Quinbury's financial situation ended in a shambles. Not having a close female friend in the household — and not able to dredge up a flirtatious mood to finagle information out of the men — she gleaned little more than a snarl of conflicting gossip. The chattiest maids had provided theories about the lord's finances that ranged from mildly possible to wildly inaccurate.

The silver must have been stolen. Perhaps that's why Peggy was let go last month.

No, it was his cousin! Wretched man thinks he's owed the money.

The estate has never been so prosperous or *He's an inch away from going belly up. What will become of us then? He'll be off to debtor's prison, and without a reference, it'll be the workhouse for me.*

Harriet had even been delivered some drivel about the lord entertaining men late at night, far too late for business deals. She discounted that when the woman named an infamous womanizer as having kept their lord company. This entire venture was a waste of breath. If Lady Katherine was so set on knowing of Lord Quinbury, Harriet would have to try again when she wasn't so consumed with the plight of a murdered woman.

In fact, she largely forgot about Lord Quinbury and the lies his staff liked to tell about him the moment the door shut behind her. She was more concerned with delivering justice to someone the rest of the world overlooked.

As she slipped through the servants' door of Mr. Blake's household and into the dim, destitute corridor, a weary sigh escaped her lips. The nearest open door led to the laundry room, and the bubble of candlelight and fatty smell of cheap candles called her inside, but her feet didn't want to move. Must she subject herself to more washing? The hour drew near to twilight. She'd hoped, by visiting the Quinbury house first, that she could avoid the laundry. As much as Gabrielle needed the help, Harriet hadn't the energy to lift a finger.

However, the glimmer of light from the room dampened Harriet's hopes. Shaking out her shoulders to banish the reluctance tightening her muscles, Harriet stepped into the doorway to greet her friend. Fortunately, the smell of lye in the room was no more than a memory. Gabrielle stood with her back turned to the door, her arms stretched over her head as she unpegged clothes from the clotheshorse. She folded them neatly as she went, sorting them into piles.

"Am I interrupting?"

Gabrielle jumped. She pressed a hand to her chest and turned to face Harriet. "You scared me near out of my skin! What are you doing here so late?" She craned her neck with a frown. "And who let you in?"

"No one heard my knock. I've been here a time or two, so I thought it best to let myself in." She'd known Gabrielle wouldn't mind. The housekeeper, had she found Harriet, might feel differently. But having been in the house before, Harriet had known the laundry room was the closest. If nothing else, she could have sought refuge in here. Not that anyone had ever sought refuge in so plain and sterile a room.

"Do you need help?" Despite her weariness, Harriet didn't have the heart to stand by and watch as her friend did all the backbreaking work without any help. Between every item Gabrielle pulled from the line, she rubbed her back, clearly weary to the bone.

"I'm nearly done."

"Why don't I pass you the clothes and you sort them?"

Gabrielle pursed her lips and cranked her eyebrows high. "In exchange for what?"

Harriet skirted the empty copper tub and set about doing precisely what she promised. Her arms didn't ache nearly so much as her feet, so she told herself it wasn't much of a trial. As she pulled down the linens, she answered in a deceptively casual voice. "Information."

"Yes, that much I gathered. But information on what?"

She'd already asked Gabrielle once, so she didn't see a point to hiding her motives. "I need to know more about Ellie Simpson."

Gabrielle gave a heart-weary sigh. "Rita—"

"—was no help at all. You say she was fast friends with Ellie, but from what I could see, she was plainly jealous."

Gabrielle raised her eyebrows, her eyes wide with disbelief. "Jealous?"

"Yes. Jealous. I'm sure it's no secret that Rita has been keeping company with Mr. Blake. I was able to find out that much without trouble."

Gabrielle wrinkled her nose. "So what if she is? He didn't give her any preferential treatment, so I don't see the harm in it."

"I never said there was any harm." Harriet frowned. "Aside from the obvious infidelity. But Rita clearly believed that Ellie was having an affair with Mr. Blake as well."

Gabrielle folded the shift in her hand with aching slowness. All the while, she canted her head to the side, considering. "I'm sure I can't say one way or another."

"You never witnessed anything between Ellie and Mr. Blake?"

As Harriet held out a pair of stockings, Gabrielle took them and rolled them into a neat ball. "Like I said, I can't say one way or another. Before Ellie..." She looked away and stuffed the ball onto a stack of clothing. "Before the accident, I didn't have cause to go about above stairs, where Ellie's duties were located. I was relegated mainly to the laundry."

Harriet's hopes shrank. She'd come here hoping that Gabrielle would have some form of information regarding Ellie's potential liaisons. In fact, she'd been hoping to prove Lyle wrong about multiple dalliances. No information, in this case, was not a good indicator.

"If not above stairs, then perhaps below stairs? Someone must have been giving Ellie gifts, and if not from the master of the house—"

Gabrielle snorted, her derision plain.

Harriet carried on over the sound. "If not from the master of the house, she must have had an admirer elsewhere. Has anyone knocked on the servants' door and asked for her in the past year?"

Gabrielle wrinkled her nose as she thought. She was so absorbed in her own thoughts that as Harriet held out the next item, a man's shirt, Gabrielle didn't so much as blink. "So many people come and go, depending on the time of day or month. Most bear messages for Mr. Blake, but Ellie or Rita are the two who deliver them. I suppose she might have come in contact with some of the messengers. I was too focused on my work to pay much mind to a maid flirting with someone who came to the door."

It was not the answer that Harriet had hoped for.

Apparently, Gabrielle could read that much on her face. She took the shirt but squeezed Harriet's hand in passing. "I know I'm not being of much help."

Harriet shrugged. "Was there anything at all you can tell me about Ellie? The only thing Rita confessed to was the fact that she wasn't here on the night Ellie was killed."

"What are you going on about? Of course she was here. Where else would she be?"

"She claimed to have gone to Brixton Hill to see her mother."

Gabrielle harrumphed. "Well, that might well be, but before that I saw her go into Ellie's room. I heard voices, so I assumed that Ellie was in there as well."

Harriet held her tongue between her teeth as she absorbed that information. "Rita told me she never saw Ellie that night." What did the lie indicate? Rats, but Lady Katherine would have known.

Did it make her a suspect? Surely Rita would not have killed a fellow maid out of jealousy for having shared their master's bed! Harriet couldn't conceive of it. A man like Mr. Blake, who didn't even spare enough coin or consideration to replace the maid he had lost, was not worth murder.

"That can't be..."

Gabrielle shrugged and folded the shirt, setting it next to a pair of men's boots. She didn't appear to have finished cleaning them.

As loath as she was to put in any real work, Gabrielle looked far worse. In fact, Harriet feared her friend was a breath away from collapsing into a heap. "You look like you're having trouble with those boots. Do you need help with them?"

Gabrielle sighed. "I'm at my wits' end. The soles are charred, and nothing I do keeps them clean for long. I swear, Mr. Blake must make a habit of kicking logs into the fire."

Harriet pressed her lips together, her eyes narrowing. "I heard he has a bad temper. Is that true?"

Gabrielle shrugged. "That's something you'll have to ask Rita, not me. Like I said, I go out of my way to avoid them upstairs. I'm far happier scrubbing out the stains than watching the cause."

A dark cloud enveloped Harriet's chest. She understood Gabrielle's sentiment all too well. Before she'd come to work for Lady Katherine, the best-paying job she'd found was as a laundry maid. And no one, not even the housekeeper, had respect for a laundry maid. Now Gabrielle was stuck doing the work of two women, not one. If Harriet could have helped in some small way, she would have.

But, since she was helpless, she let her gaze drift anywhere but to her friend. They stopped on a most curious item.

"Now what is that doing here at this time of year?"

CHAPTER TEN

If Katherine had to live for one more week in this house and watch her parents making calf eyes at each other, she would go completely and blithering mad. Even though she was more than occupied with the murder investigation and her holiday engagements, she must at all costs find the time to search out a residence of her own.

Susanna wasn't even showing her pregnancy, and yet when Katherine passed her stepmother's favorite parlor, she found Susanna lounged on the divan and her father kneeling at her feet, making what sounded like cooing sounds at her stepmother's stomach. The child was going to think he was a bird if they kept this up! The moment she found them, Katherine battled a full body shudder. She took a hasty step back.

Not soon enough. Susanna raised a hand, halting Papa's meaningless chatter at her stomach as she beckoned Katherine forward.

"Katherine, there you are! I thought you were out."

If there were any justice in this world, she would have been.

She forced a smile. "No. I have Harriet out investigating for me. I'm awaiting her return." And she couldn't come soon enough.

Papa sat back on his heels, though he didn't rise. His hand rested on Susanna's knee, possessive.

Katherine's smile felt brittle. "So sorry for intruding."

Susanna swung her legs over the side of the divan and planted her feet on the floor, pushing her husband back a pace. "You aren't intruding at all. In fact, I was looking for you earlier. We have an appointment tomorrow to inspect a townhouse in St. James's Square."

Katherine cocked her head to the side. "The one I told you about, on Charles Street?"

Susanna nodded. "The very same. The owner won't be present, but he's sending a solicitor to show us the interior."

Katherine would just as soon not meet with Lord

Conyers in any case. She smiled. "That's brilliant news."

Although she could have found a house on her own, Susanna had taken a singular delight in searching out precisely the right place for Katherine. Before marrying Papa, Susanna — a widow — had found her own such place in London and therefore had heaps of advice for Katherine. Truthfully, she was happy for the help. Not to mention Susanna's enthusiasm was infectious.

Rousted from his place by Susanna's belly, Papa unfolded himself to his full height, a few inches taller than Katherine. His piercing blue-gray eyes landed upon her, and he stroked his chin, pondering. "Katherine, if you have a moment, I'd like to speak with you in my study."

Katherine was no stranger to her father's study. In fact, it was where she had spent the greater part of her youth. Here, he had taught her the most vital aspects of investigation. Here, they had gone over countless clues, and he had fostered her mind above the silly etiquette that society insisted she learn. Nevertheless, there was a quality to his voice that turned Katherine's stomach to knots as she followed her father down the first-floor corridor and into his masculine abode. It smelled like leather and firewood, a warm and soothing scent. Papa chose one of the chairs in front of the hearth, across from the small table perpetually set with the chessboard. Katherine took the other, perching on the edge.

He ran his finger over the crown of a pawn for a long moment before he spoke. "I know Susanna is very eager to see you settled in a house of your own, but please don't let her enthusiasm fool you. You're more than welcome to stay in my house."

I know I am. Katherine opened her mouth, but her father continued over her. He moved his eyes to her, but instead of his customary shrewd gaze, for the moment they seemed limpid.

"I must confess, I'll miss you if you leave the house. I'm certain Susanna will too."

Looking into her father's earnest features, Katherine hesitated. Would it be such a chore to live in this house with the new baby? She had done it before, with her younger sisters.

But no, she wasn't leaving because her father was expecting an heir. She was leaving because she needed her independence. She had fought hard for it and didn't intend to step away from this path because it was more daunting than the complacency she found here.

She reached out to clasp Papa's hand in hers,

squeezing it. The calluses on his palm from writing brushed against her fingers. "I have to leave the nest sometime, Papa. Besides, you and Susanna deserve your privacy, don't you?"

He raised his eyebrows. "We have two children not yet grown and another on the way. What makes you think we have any privacy at all?"

She chuckled at that. "The girls are minded by their governess. It's not the same as having a grown daughter in the house, and you know it. We no longer work on the same investigations, which means if we live in the same house, we'll be likely to get in each other's way."

He sighed, pulling away from her to run his hand through his receding hair. "If that's what you want, I won't press you to stay. But I do hope you'll visit."

"Often," Katherine promised.

"Susanna tells me you're working on a case right now?"

She nodded. "It's an old case. A maid from Mr. Blake's household was found stabbed in an alley this past summer. Bow Street dismissed it as a random act of violence, but I don't think it random at all. Pru, Harriet, and I are looking into it. With Lyle's help, of course."

Papa steepled his fingers on his chin as he leaned

back in his chair. "Mr. Blake, did you say? This investigation, is that why Annandale was asking all those questions at the club?"

Katherine nodded. "Yes, he's investigating, too."

Papa's bushy eyebrows climbed toward his hairline. "Captain Wayland, as well?"

Katherine's throat closed. She clamped her hands on the arms of the chair, struggling to find her tongue.

Papa dropped his hands. "Are you working with Captain Wayland?"

"No! I would never."

Though, thinking back to the past few investigations...

No. In none of those cases had she invited his help. He'd simply shown up and offered it whether she wanted it or not.

"I mean yes, we are working on the same investigation, but not together. I promise you that."

Her father passed a hand across his face to hide what must be a grimace. He certainly couldn't be smirking at her! Though it appeared for a second as if that was what he was hiding.

But why would he smirk? Papa disdained Wayland. He would undoubtedly think less of her for accepting help from such a source. *Would he? Why?* Katherine gritted her teeth. From everything Wayland had shown her thus far, he was an intelligent, capable detective, perhaps even of higher morals in his investigation practices than she. Still, she'd rather be rid of him. She disliked him as much her father…

Didn't she? Every time they were together, they butted heads and exchanged quips, trying to finagle information out of each other. It had been that way since her first solo investigation. But was her opinion born of experience, or had her presumptions about him been colored by her father's complaints about him?

What *had* Papa said, precisely? Nothing specific that Katherine's impeccable memory could recall. However, Katherine was adept at reading between the lines. If Papa disliked him, he had a reason—

And now Papa was staring at her, waiting for her explanation. Hadn't she given him one already? He lowered his hand from his mouth, his expression impenetrable.

"Papa, you know I would never work with Wayland. I know you don't wish for me to. The only reason I've been seeing more of him lately is because… Because of Pru! Pru tells Lord Annandale about all of our investigations, and he's Wayland's closest friend and—"

Papa laughed. "Since when do you ever do as I wish?"

Katherine stared at him, agape. She tried to be the dutiful daughter. If perhaps she was a little bit stubborn, the trait served her well in her chosen occupation.

At the flabbergasted look on her face, the corners of his mouth quirked upwards. He crossed one ankle over the other. "Why don't you tell me about this investigation you're conducting?"

Thankful for the change in topic, Katherine let out a slow breath. "The very first thing I discovered was that Ellie Simpson, the maid who was stabbed, possessed articles of clothing and jewelry that no maid could afford. We've been following that clue for the moment, and I have Harriet off to the Blake household as we speak to ask the servants if Ellie had any paramours outside of the house. We don't think Mr. Blake would have given her those things, seeing as he is rather stingy with his money."

Papa nodded. "And?"

"And there are various other factors, as well. We're not only looking at a potential lover for the crime, even though I think it is the most likely outcome. Mr. Blake has a reputation for taking his maids to bed." Katherine didn't hesitate to mention the sordid details, considering that they had worked on dozens of investigations together. Since the men and women involved were rarely saints, Katherine had learned of this side to life young. "Rita, another maid in Mr. Blake's household, is certainly one of them, and it's possible she was jealous if Ellie was a second. If Mr. Blake did provide those gifts to Ellie, both Rita and his wife had motive for jealousy. I have it on good authority that he never showers his wife with gifts. I don't know enough at the moment to be able to point to one suspect over another, but I'm hoping that Harriet will return soon with some news."

Papa nodded. "You have a good head on your shoulders, and you're making good deductions. But, pumpkin, don't forget that things are not always as they seem."

Katherine frowned. In terms of the investigation, she thought she was looking at the clues from all angles. But from the way he spoke, it almost sounded as if his words had a double meaning. Whatever could he mean?

He stood, rolling back his shoulders. "You'd best get ready. Susanna and I will be leaving for the New Year's ball soon."

Katherine made a face. "I forgot about that. Will you give my excuses? I must meet up with Pru"—and Wayland, Annandale and McTavish—"to exchange news of this investigation."

Papa held her gaze a moment more before he

nodded solemnly. "I'll give your excuses to the hosts. Dazzle *her* with your brilliance, my dear," he added with a wink.

Almost as though he'd guessed she was meeting with more people than Pru alone.

CHAPTER ELEVEN

With the house to herself, Katherine paced the first-floor parlor. Emma trotted at her heels, the clicking of her little claws on the floor periodically muffled as she passed across the rug. Katherine turned and nearly tripped over Pru, who was lounged in a chaise with her feet stretched in front of her. Katherine hopped over her ankles and stumbled a couple of steps before she continued her brisk tour of the room.

"Where is she?" Katherine mumbled under her breath.

Click-click, click-click.

Loudly, Pru complained, "Why are we waiting? If we don't leave soon, we'll be late to the meeting. Don't you want to meet with the others to compare notes?"

Katherine spun to face her. "I do." However, she craved the information Harriet had to provide more.

Her stomach clenched. What if Harriet wasn't back yet because she hadn't been able to find anything? At this rate, Katherine would have precious little to exchange with Wayland in order to discover what he knew.

No, Harriet couldn't have failed. She was far too gregarious a person. She made friends like Katherine collected books, finding one in nearly every household in London.

"Harriet will return soon."

"So you said half an hour ago."

Katherine gritted her teeth and glanced at the open door. From her vantage point in the parlor, she could see the staircase and beyond, on the ground floor, the front door leading onto the street. It remained resolutely closed.

"I know I did, but I promised her I would wait. She's out to find information for us, information we can use."

Pru lifted a finger. "Wouldn't it be better to go to the meeting first, in that case? Then after, we'll know something the others do not. As it is, we're set to exchange all information on the investigation."

Katherine lifted her eyebrows at her friend. "Do

you truly think they will be impressed with what little we've discovered thus far?"

"How do you know they've found more than us?"

She didn't, of course. However, she had the irritating and perhaps irrational fear that Wayland had outdone her. Worse than the thought of acting the marriage-mad fool during a ball was the idea that she would lose to *Wayland*. At all costs, she had to prove that she was his equal, perhaps even his better at investigation. That would be the only way he would stop discounting her theories the moment they came out of her mouth.

She clenched her fists.

Emma yipped. Katherine jumped as the dog bolted out of the room, the sound of her departure echoing in the stillness. A moment later, Harriet's laugh drifted in from the corridor, though its source remained out of view. Katherine rushed to the door, determined to meet her at once.

With a broad smile, Harriet scooped Emma into her arms and rearranged the bow around her neck. "Did you miss me, girl?"

"You're back. When did you arrive?" Katherine glanced at the door down the stairs, reassuring herself that it was, indeed, shut. It hadn't opened. She'd been keeping too close an eye on it.

Harriet raised one eyebrow in a supercilious expression. "I came in the servants' door, as always."

Why hadn't Katherine thought of that? They could have waited in the kitchen. She lunged into the corridor, catching Harriet by the sleeve and towing her into the parlor. "Quick, tell me what you've learned. We're set to leave for Lord Annandale's townhouse at any moment."

"I had a lot of time to think on the walk home. Near as I can tell, Lord Quinbury must be in financial trouble. Either that, or he's battling some sticky-fingered servants."

Katherine frowned. For a moment, she'd forgotten that she'd sent Harriet out on two investigative tasks. As much as she wanted to tell Harriet to forget this until tomorrow, better she committed to memory now.

"What makes you say that?"

Harriet tipped Emma over in her arms and started to rub her belly. As the pug wriggled in glee, she answered, "He's been letting go of his staff. There's talk in the house that maybe one of them stole the silver and pawned it, but if that were the case, Lord Quinbury would have simply bought it back. That leads me to believe he must be in financial trouble. I'd have to go back in order to find something more concrete..."

Katherine waved her hand. "It might be enough." If she could find a way to slip that information to Miss Graylocke's parents, perhaps it would be enough to dissuade them from the match. Of course, Katherine had scarcely spoken a word to them in her life. They might not trust her as an advisor. She had to find a subtler way of providing them the information.

That was a problem for another day. She waved her hand, indicating for Harriet to carry on. "What did you discover at Mr. Blake's?"

Immediately, Harriet averted her gaze. She set Emma on the ground and straightened to brush the dog hair off her frock. She didn't look Katherine in the eye.

"Did you find something?"

Harriet's gaze, when she lifted it, was sly. "Oh, I found something."

"Well, what is it?" Pru asked, impatient. She rose from the chaise and stormed closer. "We haven't got the time to tease it out of you."

It was the wrong way to deal with Harriet, as Katherine well knew. The moment the words left Pru's mouth, Harriet crossed her arms over her chest and lifted her chin, stubborn. "Shouldn't you be asking me something else, instead?"

"Like what?" Katherine asked.

At the same time Pru answered, "No."

The glare didn't make its way to Harriet's face, but she pointedly shifted her position to cut Pru out of the conversation. Looking Katherine directly in the eye, she said, "You should ask me to come along."

Katherine raised her thumbnail to her mouth, nibbling on it. Why was Harriet so insistent on coming along? She seemed fixated on being incorporated into every part of this investigation, when usually she fought her hardest to stay out of the matter.

"You let that Scottish oaf McTavish into your meetings, don't you? So why can't I come, too?"

"McTavish happens to be a valet in that household. He is there because he has nowhere else to be."

Pru's voice might have been a trick of the wind for all the attention Harriet gave her. She drove the final nail into the coffin when she added, "If you'd like to know what I discovered today, you'll have to bring me with you. I'm not about to tell you what I learned from my friend until I'm sitting in Lord Annandale's parlor, discussing the matter with everyone at once."

Katherine nodded, but Harriet didn't appear to be paying the least bit of attention to her.

She brushed down the front of her dress and frowned. "I must change clothes so I don't smell of lye.

Even better, what if the men come here, to Dorchester House?"

At that, Katherine balked. "My father—"

"—won't find out. Isn't he at the New Year's ball tonight? He'll be there until after one of the morning at the earliest."

To Katherine's surprise, Pru smirked and embraced the idea. "Yes, let's invite them here. I know my Annandale won't mind, and what do you care if Wayland does?"

"I don't."

"Then it's settled." Having been at Dorchester House many times over the past few months, Pru stormed towards the writing desk and opened the drawer containing the parchment. She grabbed all the accoutrements for writing and began penning a note to her fiancé. "Do you have any footmen on duty to deliver this?"

"I'll check," Harriet promised. She pointed a finger at Katherine. "Then I'll change my clothes, and we'll have to hurry if we hope to prepare."

"Prepare for what?"

Harriet threw her hands in the air. "What do you think? The new year!"

THEY ALMOST CERTAINLY HAD SERVANTS FOR this. However, Katherine swallowed her protests, and for the first time in their acquaintance, she answered Harriet's command as she, Harriet, and Pru set about cleaning the house. As she swept the last of the imaginary dirt — she was certain the servants had already done this today — out the back door, thereby sweeping out any lingering negativity from the year, she straightened. She sighed as the ache in her back eased.

"What time is it? It feels as if we have been going about this for hours."

Harriet scoffed. "It wasn't very much work. An hour at most."

"An hour! Why haven't Wayland and Annandale arrived yet?"

Surprisingly, Pru didn't look worried. When Katherine fixed her gaze on her friend, Pru's eyes widened. "Don't look at me, I haven't the faintest idea."

Katherine had been trained by her father to detect lies in those she questioned. Even a child could have told from Pru's tone that she knew precisely why Annandale and Wayland hadn't yet arrived. As she opened her mouth to protest, the stroke of a clock shattered the silence in the house.

Clang, clang, clang.

The grandfather clock was joined by other, smaller pieces throughout the house in a symphony of ringing of bells.

Was it midnight?

Pru clutched Katherine by the hand and towed her through the house toward the front. Seeing as she was more than ready to sit down again, Katherine didn't protest. Between the three of them, they had not only swept the house, but had put on a pot of wassail to warm in the kitchen.

At last, the twelfth chime rang resonated, growing dim. The sound of Katherine's footsteps sounded overly loud in the silence as Pru hauled her into the foyer in time to intercept a knock at the door. *At last.* The moment Pru released her, Katherine reached for the handle.

"If this isn't the men, we're going to have words about that note you sent."

Pru batted her hands. "Open it!"

Katherine swung the door wide to reveal three mountainous men — Lord Annandale and McTavish standing behind Wayland, their heads visible over his shoulders. Snow clung to their heads and shoulders, dusting the dark greatcoats they wore. Without a word or invitation, Wayland stepped into her house.

CHAPTER TWELVE

Katherine took the smallest of steps back to make room for Wayland, but it felt like a retreat. She straightened her spine and opened her mouth, but she didn't know whether she was about to redress him or formally invite him and the other men inside the house. She found the chance to do neither. From behind, Pru clamped her hand over Katherine's mouth, stifling her words.

Wayland looked a bit sheepish, his shoulders rounded and his hands tucked into his pockets. He gave her a halfhearted shrug and said, "Happy new year."

Pru released Katherine's mouth. She turned, glaring at her friend, who didn't look repentant in the least. From the parlor, Emma erupted in a series of happy barks as she scrambled forward to greet Wayland. She jumped on her hind legs, planting her front paws near his knee as she begged him for attention. He didn't take his eyes off of Katherine's.

"Happy new year," she answered, irritated and breathless. This year was starting in an extremely bizarre manner.

It only grew more peculiar from there. Lord Annandale nudged Wayland's elbow, giving him an enthusiastic nod.

Whatever that was about, they must have rehearsed it, because Wayland tucked his hands into his greatcoat pockets. He emerged with a bundle wrapped in a handkerchief. "I have gifts."

Katherine frowned. "Why?"

Lord Annandale grinned. "It's tradition, lass."

Not any tradition she practiced. However, she accepted the handkerchief and waved everyone inside. Once Lord Annandale and McTavish stepped free of the door, they revealed a fourth, lankier man in their wake. Katherine smiled without reserve. "Lyle! I didn't know if you would make it, with your work schedule."

He shrugged as he tapped his boots to rid them of snow and stepped into the house. "Call me curious." When he jerked his chin towards the handkerchief in her hand, Katherine couldn't decide whether he was more curious about the investigation or about the gift she'd been given.

"Must I open it in the foyer, or can we move into the parlor? It's dreadfully cold with the door open."

Wayland, for whatever reason, glanced at Lord Annandale for the answer. The big man shrugged. "The parlor will do. But do not tarry, we have an investigation to discuss."

Nodding, Katherine stepped back and beckoned everyone forward. As Wayland kneeled to pay homage to Emma, setting something behind him, Harriet squeezed in between those gathering and collected everyone's cloaks. As she reached McTavish, standing close to Lyle, she raised her gaze. "I see you came as well."

He grinned. "I could nae miss this, could I?" He handed over his greatcoat and gloves without protest. Harriet struggled a bit under the weight of everyone's outer garments but pressed her lips into a thin line and continued to Lyle.

As she gave McTavish one last, lingering glare, his smile widened. "I hear you've been dabbling in the investigation yourself, lass. If you ever need some advice—"

Lyle forgotten, Harriet straightened and glared at McTavish, never mind that she only reached as high as his chest. "I think I would be the one to give *you* advice. After all, I've been doing this far longer than you have."

The air between them crackled with tension. Katherine had been right to suspect a rivalry between the two, even if she couldn't decide when it had been born. McTavish grinned at Harriet with the same flirtatious look he gave to half the female population. More puzzling ... did Harriet return it?

His expression forbidding, Lyle stepped between the pair, turning his back to McTavish. "Those look heavy. Let me help you, Harriet."

Grudgingly, Harriet let him relieve her of the weight. Lyle stood a bit taller as he accompanied her to the hooks in the back room where she would hang the clothes to dry. Could Lyle be jealous of the attention Harriet gave McTavish?

No. Katherine had been taking on too many matchmaking jobs. They were befuddling her mind.

As Harriet and Lyle disappeared towards the servants' wing on the ground floor, Katherine led her guests up the stairs to the same parlor where she had awaited Harriet's return. The hearth was cold, at Harriet's insistence that it not be lit until after the clocks chimed midnight. Katherine was thankful her maid hadn't insisted on the candles being snuffed as well. She set her gift on the mantel and knelt to take care of the fire in the hearth. It wasn't a task she did herself often, but it couldn't be too taxing to light a flame from the tinderbox. As she reached for the box, also on the mantel, Lord Annandale interrupted her.

"Open your gift first, lass."

The chill had started to creep into her bones, born from the cold air let in by the men. However, she readjusted her shawl and reached for the handkerchief without protest.

She unfolded it to reveal an eclectic array of gifts.

"What on earth?" She stared at the gifts. A shilling, a lump of coal the size of her fist, a piece of shortbread smaller than her palm, what looked like a pinch of salt, and a black bun.

"This, too," Wayland said as he offered one last gift. He held out a bottle of amber whiskey. The label was Scottish. At a guess, he'd pilfered it from Annandale's stash.

He shrugged sheepishly as she accepted it. "It didn't fit in the handkerchief."

"Thank you," she answered, more from years of etiquette training than anything else. "But these have to be the most bizarre gifts I've ever received."

Wayland looked every bit as baffled at them as she

did. She turned her attention to the one man who seemed to know the reason for the gifts.

"It's tradition," Lord Annandale answered to the inquisitive raise of her eyebrows, as if that explained everything.

It did not.

At her blank look, he raised his gaze heavenward as if praying for patience. He smoothed his well-groomed beard. "The first man through the door on the new year has to provide the host gifts that represent" —he counted items off on his fingers— "financial prosperity, warmth, food, good cheer, and flavor for the new year."

"If it's so important that these gifts are provided, why didn't you give them?"

A funny feeling wrapped her chest as she pictured Wayland fighting Lord Annandale for the honor. A pugilist match, perhaps, or a race.

Bluntly, Annandale answered, "My feet aren't the right shape."

On second thought, perhaps she ought not to ask more about the business.

"Why don't you sit down? I'll tend to the fire, and we'll begin when Harriet and Lyle return."

However, when she reached for the tinderbox, Wayland took it from her. His expression was impassive, and looking far surer of himself than when he'd given her the gifts, he told her, "I'll take care it for you. I think you're meant to burn the coal."

Thrown so off-balance by this entire exchange, Katherine stepped back and let him take the liberty of lighting her fire. The other men in the room remained standing, although Pru had found a loveseat for her and Lord Annandale to sit in. Katherine supposed that the men, practicing good manners, would remain standing until she chose a chair as well. She sat in a plain armchair near the hearth and patted her lap to beckon Emma closer.

Instead, the traitorous dog trotted at Wayland's heels, still begging for his attention. Katherine scowled but pretended she didn't notice.

Harriet and Lyle returned a moment later, the former carrying a silver serving tray laden with seven steaming cups. The moment she entered, McTavish turned to her with a gleam in his eye. "That looks a mite heavy fer you, lass. Why don't I take it off yer hands?"

"I have it." She tugged the tray away from him when he reached for it. Sidestepping him neatly, she set it down on the table. She waved everyone to their seats. "Sit down, and I'll have these out in a trice."

McTavish filched two cups from the tray and added, "I'll help. It'll go faster."

Indeed, it went extremely fast. Harriet seemed to be competing with McTavish to dole out the most cups. In the end, he only served his master and Pru before turning back to a tray that held only enough cups for him and Harriet. He took them both and, with a wink, handed her one. She took it from him grudgingly, then retreated to the edge of the settee nearest to Katherine.

Katherine had had more than enough of competition for one night. Weary, she peered across the room at Wayland, who had claimed the other armchair, next to Lyle on the far end of the settee from Harriet.

Katherine warmed her hands with her cup as she asked, "How are your inquiries at the club faring?"

Lord Annandale spluttered on his wassail. "How do ye know we were asking 'round at the club?"

Katherine leaned back in her chair, smiling in satisfaction. "I have my ways."

She thought she caught Wayland smirking, but when she looked at him directly, his face was composed. This time, instead of finagling her for information, he offered up his own without protest.

"From everything we've uncovered, Mr. Blake is not what you would consider a saint, nor even a gentleman. He has lovers aplenty in his household and out of it, and I suspect he is involved in smuggling silk, lace, brandy, or all three."

Lyle straightened. He removed a small notebook out of his pocket and opened it to a new page. He dabbed the end of a graphite pencil to his tongue before perching over the page. "I don't suppose you have any details on the smuggling?"

Wayland wrinkled his nose. "I'm afraid I don't. All I've heard is that he has a warehouse along the Thames..." Wayland looked pondering as he took a sip from his cup. Emma seemed to take that as an invitation, because she jumped into his lap and curled into a comfortable ball. Katherine gritted her teeth at the pug's blatant preference.

"Actually," Wayland answered, "I think the warehouse is down the street from the Hound and Ale Pub, the establishment struck by lightning and burned the night of the murder."

Harriet tapped her toe. *Rap-tap-tap, rap-tap-tap.* "Do you think Mr. Blake could have killed Ellie? Perhaps he tired of her and she protested."

"Doubtful," McTavish drawled. Somehow, he'd managed to position himself between Harriet and Lyle. Neither seemed particularly pleased with him, and not only because McTavish's large body stretched across the bulk of the settee as he draped his arms across the back. In that casual pose, he tipped his head to Harriet. "He'd nae have a reason to kill her. A wee scrap of a maid would nae cause him any trouble simply if he didn't want to take her to bed anymore. No offense, Harriet." McTavish smiled, a welcoming expression that said he counted himself her equal when referencing class.

It didn't seem to mollify her. Sourly, Harriet bit out, "None taken."

Pru added, "What if she had more than one lover? Mr. Blake could have been jealous and killed her because of it."

At that, Wayland laughed. "Trust me, Mr. Blake is not the kind of man to care. He has women in every corner of London. One maid offering herself to another man won't bother him one way or another."

Katherine frowned, hiding it behind a sip of her wassail. How could Wayland possibly know that? From experience? The heirs of titled lords often caroused through London, taking women left, right, and center — and disposing of them when they grew bored. However, Katherine had never considered Wayland to be that sort of man. Was she wrong? Did he have women squirreled away in London, the same as Mr. Blake?

And why did that thought make her uncomfortable?

Fortunately, no one — least of all Wayland — realized her discomfort. He continued, "You might be on the right track though, in spirit. Annandale and I have come to the conclusion that the killer might be one of Mr. Blake's other lovers who was jealous of Ellie. And killed her to get her out of the way."

Sullenly, Katherine mumbled, "We came to that conclusion two days ago."

He raised an eyebrow in her direction. "Does it matter who concluded the matter when? I thought our wager was about who could figure out the killer first, not the reason."

Katherine forced herself to unclench her jaw. Reluctantly, she admitted, "It was. And I must say, I agree with you. I don't think Mr. Blake tired of Ellie or killed her out of jealousy. When we spoke with Ellie's sister, she told us that she saw Ellie entering a carriage with Mr. Blake's crest on the door. At first, I thought he loaned it to her, but it makes far more sense if he was in the carriage, awaiting her. He certainly wouldn't be driving around with her if he'd tired of her or she'd thrown him over for someone else."

The men around the room nodded. All save for

Lyle, who seemed consumed by thought. Abruptly, he asked, "Is Mr. Blake right-handed?"

Everyone turned to stare at him, frowning. He looked up from his notebook, seeming to return from whatever thought process had taken him away from the conversation. He smiled, sheepishly.

Slowly, Wayland answered, "Yes. I believe I saw him sign something at the club. He is right-handed. Why?"

Lyle tapped his notes. "The way the wounds were described on the victim, I believe she must have been stabbed by a right-handed person."

Katherine sighed. *Tarnation.* That information did little to narrow their suspect pool.

Seeming to hear Katherine's thoughts and agree with them, Wayland stroked Emma's rump as he mused. "That leaves ninety percent of the population as suspects." For all that he'd argued with her deductions initially, they seemed to have realigned their thoughts.

Had they been working on the same team, that would have been to the better. Alas, if he was apt to deduce the same things she did, she would have to work harder to win this wager.

"May I tell you what I learned today?" Harriet asked. The tapping of her foot ceased as the room turned to her. Katherine had forgotten about the new, interesting clue that Harriet claimed to have found.

She leaned forward and nodded. "By all means, please do."

Smug, Harriet patted down her skirts. "I went to Mr. Blake's house to learn more from a friend about Ellie. I was hoping to find she'd taken an additional lover, but unfortunately my friend wasn't able to help me in that case. However, she did tell me that when Ellie was home earlier the day she was killed, Rita — another maid and lover of Mr. Blake's — entered her room and spoke to her. I was told the two were friendly and often chatted, but when I spoke with Rita, she seemed more jealous than anything else."

Katherine frowned, mulling this information over.

Harriet added, "But that's not all." Smug as a mouse in the cheese, she added, "Mrs. Blake might be having an affair with her driver!"

McTavish straightened from his casual position. He frowned, skeptical. "What makes you think that, lass? Do you have proof? Could be the maid was lying or 'tis no more than idle gossip."

Harriet sat as straight as a pole, glaring at him. "I know what I'm doing when I investigate. I can sniff out a clue as good as anyone else."

"Of course you can," said Lyle, somewhat molli-fying her.

Hoping to defuse the situation, Katherine added, "Please, tell us more."

Harriet smiled, satisfied. "Well, you see, my friend had a pair of shoes she was working on in the laundry. Well, two pairs of shoes. One belonged to Mr. Blake — I take it he has a problem with his temper and likes to kick the logs in the fire. But in any case, next to them was a pair of lovely, embroidered silk shoes. They were water-stained, and my friend was making a futile attempt to get the stains out. Trust me, it's a nearly impossible task. Anyway, she informed me that Mrs. Blake had soiled them while running in from one of her clandestine trips to the livery."

Frowning, Pru asked, "Why would Mrs. Blake make a clandestine trip to the livery?"

"Only one reason. To see the livery driver without anyone else knowing." Whenever Katherine called for a carriage, she sent the footman to see that the vehicle was readied and brought around to the front door. Pru was right: Mrs. Blake didn't have any reason to visit the livery. And if she didn't have a valid reason, that could only mean she went to see the driver. Perhaps Harriet was right. "Lady Dalhousie mentioned something about Mrs. Blake having as much of a wandering eye as her husband."

"Do you think the driver would have the funds to buy a gold bracelet?"

McTavish snorted. "Gold? Nay, lass. Not if he makes the pittance I do."

Across the room, Lord Annandale grunted, displeased. "Perhaps if you learned to curtail your mouth, you'd earn a pittance more."

Pru hid a smile behind her hand.

Before this devolved into some petty squabble, Katherine explained, "You see, Ellie's sister told me that she had a silver bracelet with a ruby clasp in the shape of a heart. I thought Mr. Blake might have given it to her—"

Wayland shook his head, lending his opinion of her theory. She ignored him.

"—so I conspired to get a look at Mrs. Blake's wrist. She was hiding a bracelet, but not the one described by Ellie's sister. Her husband never buys her jewelry, so it must have been given to her by someone else."

She tapped her lips, following the thread of her theory aloud.

"Perhaps it wasn't pure gold, but merely gold-plated. I didn't get close enough to examine it for quality. She hid it too quickly. Lady Dalhousie told me that

Mrs. Blake enjoys money. I wonder if she could have persuaded the driver to buy her the bracelet as a token of his affection. That would give her motive to want to keep it hidden, wouldn't it?"

Lyle pointed out, "If she likes money so well, she might have purchased it for herself. Surely she would have access to some funds. If Mr. Blake didn't care for her spending his money, that could be why she kept it hidden. What does this have to do with the murder?"

Wayland nodded. "Nothing, I'd say. If Mrs. Blake was having her own affair and her lover bought her jewelry, she would hardly kill the maid because she was jealous of her husband. In fact, she would probably encourage her husband to be otherwise occupied so he wouldn't notice that she was having an affair as well."

Katherine fought hard not to scowl, but the only grudging word she could part from her thinned lips was, "Perhaps."

Wayland took it for encouragement. "And if she bought the bracelet for herself, it would have no bearing on the death of her maid."

"We wondered if she might have pawned Ellie's bracelet to get funds for her own," Katherine said through gritted teeth.

This he allowed with a gracious nod of his head. "We can check the pawn shops tomorrow."

"I've already gone. I found nothing, and the shop-keepers weren't forthcoming." She hated to admit her failure. It made her theory even more inconsequential.

If Harriet had told her of this news before spilling it to everyone at once, Katherine might have been able to vent her thoughts and deduce Wayland's conclusion on her own. Then she wouldn't be left feeling like his inferior. Whatever else he was, he was also an astute detective. And he was right.

Lord Annandale drained his cup of wassail and set it on his knee. "Och now, if it is not Mrs. Blake who was jealous, it must be one of Mr. Blake's other lovers. We need more clues!"

Wayland nodded, but he didn't appear entirely convinced. "Sometimes, the key to an investigation is in the small details. Let's think about what we know. We might find a clue among it. Something someone said or did..."

Harriett snapped her fingers. "Wait a minute. The other maid, Rita, lied. She told me she was at her mother's cottage in Brixton during the storm. But my friend saw her with Ellie before the murder. She couldn't possibly have driven all the way there in time!"

Dubious, McTavish muttered, "Why would she lie?"

Pru suggested, "Perhaps because she is the killer."

Lord Annandale grunted but didn't appear to have confidence in Pru's suggestion. Perhaps because McTavish added, "I met with wee Rita. She's a mite small to be stabbing people in the middle of alleys."

Katherine glared at him, but unfortunately none of the men came to the defense of the idea.

In fact, Lord Annandale cracked a yawn, hiding it behind his hand as he suggested, "Perhaps we ought to sleep on this before we exchange more information. 'Tis a lot to think about. If you do nae mind, 'tis high time I took my leave."

Katherine raised her gaze to the clock in the room, finding that they had spoken for nearly an hour. Papa might return at any minute! No matter the cost, he couldn't find Wayland in his home. Katherine jumped to her feet. "I'll find someone to order the carriage."

When she did, the other men rose as well, McTavish included.

"No need, lass. I'll do it myself. I know the way." He strode out of the room, downstairs, where he likely went in search of his greatcoat. Harriet didn't seem particularly keen to follow, so Katherine figured he couldn't do much harm if left to his own devices.

After a moment spent collecting everyone's cups, Harriet settled them all on the tray and told everyone to wait while she fetched the cloaks, Pru's included. Katherine led them down to wait by the door for their outer clothes, but Lord Annandale blocked it, shaking his head.

"We have to leave out the back."

Katherine stifled a sigh. "Another tradition?"

He nodded.

Fortunately, Harriet was quick. She met them partway as Katherine led the group down the narrow servants' corridor. It was barely wide enough for the men's shoulders, and they had to walk in single file. Katherine led the way, with Wayland on her heels and Harriet taking up the rear to keep Emma in line. Although she didn't look behind her, Katherine felt the vibrations from Wayland's every step.

As they reached the kitchen, she paused, her gaze fixed on a bough of mistletoe hanging on the threshold of the kitchen door. *Tarnation!* She'd forgotten this was here. Three plump berries taunted her from the crux of the leaves. The bough called for three more kisses to be bestowed as couples crossed the threshold at once, lest bad luck befall them on the year ahead. She didn't much care about superstition, but Harriet did, and the fuss Harriet would make should she attempt to walk beneath without acknowledging the mistletoe promised to be mortifying.

Not to mention, although she wasn't superstitious, she didn't know if Wayland was. If he believed in the silly reign of bad luck, he might decide to kiss her! There had been a time, in Bath, when she'd thought he wanted to... But it was better for them all that she'd been mistaken.

When she glanced over her shoulder, she found him looking at the mistletoe with indecision. Her heartbeat stuttered, and her mouth dried. Surely he didn't intend to kiss her! Not here, in front of everyone.

Not at all.

Leaning forward, Lord Annandale jostled Wayland into Katherine as he plucked two berries from the bough. The breath rushed from her chest as Wayland's body collided with hers, pressing her back against the wall. With a look of irritation, Wayland levered himself away from her to glare at Lord Annandale.

Paying no mind to his friend, Lord Annandale thrust his arm between them to capture her hand. "My apologies, lass." He bestowed a kiss on her knuckles before turning to his wife-to-be and kissing her full on the mouth. Pru sank into the kiss, unashamed to be sharing it with him in front of such an audience.

Her insides squirming, Katherine turned away to give them privacy.

When they parted, she brushed down the front of her gown and tried not to recall that everyone had seen Wayland press against her. It hadn't been the first time — their investigations together had thus far put them in a variety of private situations, particularly in Bath — but heretofore, they had never shared such moments with their friends. Although she tried to avoid Wayland's gaze, she couldn't miss his expression in her peripheral vision. He stood in the threshold of the door, looking at her askance.

The very last thing she would do was kiss him! However, when she turned to sharpen her tongue at him, no more berries hid between the leaves of mistletoe. Had she miscounted? She must have. In any case, it was safe to walk beneath.

Her stomach shriveled into a raisin. She couldn't define the lingering emotion behind the sensation. Embarrassment, perhaps. Certainly not disappointment. Without a word, she led the men to the back door and bid them good night without looking at them.

Lyle, the last to depart, left with his face a bright scarlet red.

CHAPTER THIRTEEN

As Katherine followed Harriet through the ankle-deep snow, she wished for her cloak. However, her clothing had been far too expensive to pass for that of a servant and her red cloak too noticeable. Despite her argument that perhaps she could claim the garment was a castoff from her fictional mistress, Harriet had insisted that they borrow clothes from the maids in Dorchester House, none of whom happened to be tall enough to wear gowns or cloaks that covered Katherine's ankles. However, Harriet had been firm. If Katherine did not dress the part, she would have been relegated to waiting at the house while Harriet continued to investigate.

This time, Katherine refused to do any such thing.

Even Pru had been willing to put aside her pride and don the thinner clothing.

"Maybe we should visit the scene of the crime first," Katherine said under her breath. "Someone might have seen Rita there, and that would solidify our case."

"First let's see for ourselves what Rita has to say. I know you will be able to make her slip up if she's guilty. We can visit the place where Ellie was killed later on if need be. It's not like there will be any evidence left lying around. Besides, the murder happened months ago, and people's memories are short," Pru said.

"I can't believe Wayland and Lord Annandale discounted our theory that Rita might be the killer! Size doesn't mean anything if one has a sharp enough blade. I suppose McTavish is besotted," Harriet said, glancing back at Pru. Katherine agreed with the statement but wondered if Harriet was hinting around to find out if her theory on McTavish being besotted was true.

Pru shrugged, but whatever she and Lord Annandale had spoken of after leaving Katherine's house last night — or, she should say, early this morning — she refused to speak a word of it. Katherine sighed, dropping the subject as Mr. Blake's house came into view.

"If not the killer, she lied, so she knows something," Katherine said. "And I aim to find out what it is."

Whatever Rita was hiding could be the very thing that broke the case. She could very well be the killer, and if Katherine could get a confession today, she would win the wager they'd set. And, as the icing atop the cake, she would see both Wayland and Lord Annandale tomorrow night at the monthly meeting of the Royal Society for Investigative Techniques. She would get him to acknowledge that she was the better detective in a room full of their peers.

When Katherine would have stepped up to the front door, Harriet clasped her arm and led her down a steep flight of steps to a discreet door at the back of the house. "We'll enter here. Gabrielle, my friend, works in the laundry room closest to this door. We should be able to find her without too much trouble." She waited for Katherine to nod before she knocked on the door. As agreed, Katherine let Harriet take the lead. Katherine looked enough like her father that she feared being recognized if she led the way into the house. Not to mention, Harriet had friends here and would be able to more easily gain entrance.

"A moment," said a muffled voice from within. The door was opened by a short woman with a weary expression. Upon seeing Harriet, her eyes widened and her mouth slackened in relief as she shoved a pile of white linen onto her hip and out of her face. However, the moment her gaze traveled from beyond Harriet to Katherine, her expression shuttered once more.

"Good morning, Gabrielle. We're here—"

Gabrielle turned away. "If you'll tell no one I'm the one who let you into the house, I've no need to know why you're here."

Katherine exchanged a wary glance with Pru before stepping into the narrow corridor. There was only room enough for one of them to walk abreast. She took her lead from Harriet and stamped the snow off her shoes before following the maid into a nearby room.

In this cramped, barren room, the interior was lit with a sole tallow candle. The air smelled sharply of something that bit into Katherine's nostrils. She wrinkled her nose and breathed shallowly through her mouth, blinking rapidly. The vapor in the air was enough to sting.

"We're hoping to talk to Rita."

Gabrielle piled the linens into a steaming basin and shoved at them with the nearby stick, making certain that every stray corner was submerged. Only then did she turn to look not at Harriet but directly at Katherine.

"You're certain she was killed, and this wasn't an accident."

Katherine raised her eyebrows. "Ellie Simpson was stabbed in the middle of the street."

Gabrielle grimaced. "I knew that, of course. But bad things happen in certain parts of town and..."

"It was not a random murder," Katherine said softly. "We haven't uncovered the culprit yet for certain, but Rita could be the clue that brings the matter to light."

Her expression souring, Gabrielle lowered her eyes and stared into the basin. "Very well, my lady. Rita was helping me to strip off the coverlets upstairs. She'll be down at any moment."

Katherine fought not to sigh at the formal address. Why did she have to be so darn tall? Her height and figure made her far too easily recognizable. Still, she held the faint hope that Harriet's friend had only known her because she'd been with Harriet.

The laundry maid stepped back, still not meeting Katherine's gaze. "You can wait here, but I'm making myself scarce. I want no part in whatever you're doing."

Katherine didn't stop her. She didn't miss the

pained expression on Harriet's face, either. How close were Harriet and Gabrielle? She'd never stopped to think about the consequences of her investigations on Harriet's friendships. Guilt warred with affection. Harriet was loyal to a fault, but Katherine would have to consider the tasks she sent her on more carefully. She didn't want to jeopardize the other woman's friendships.

We're doing vital work. It was the truth, and yet Katherine couldn't decide whether or not it made up for the strained relationship Harriet would no doubt have with Gabrielle after this business was concluded.

If they had to wait, Katherine preferred not to do it in a room that made her eyes water. She turned her gaze to the floor because it made them sting less and turned to leave. As she did, she spotted the man's burned boots and the embroidered silk shoes with water stains that Harriet had described.

The shoes were indeed lovely. Blue satin with embroidered flowers. Too bad a water stain spread in an ugly blotch over the tops—the very part that would be seen the most. Katherine thought about Mrs. Blake running out to the livery. A woman having a fling with her driver would hardly be jealous of a maid her husband was bedding, not to mention that apparently, Mrs. Blake had her own admirer giving her jewelry, if the way she took pains to hide that gold bracelet was any indication.

Katherine's choice of footwear was much more practical, especially in winter, but still she had never paid much mind to her shoes. Did Harriet spend hours trying to get stains out of hers?

Gabrielle scurried out of sight, up a servants' stair. As she did, Katherine dismissed the shoes and turned to those of Mr. Blake. His boots undoubtedly took precedence, given that he was the master of the house, but it sounded as though he kicked the logs and burned his shoes so often that Gabrielle had no time to work on those of Mrs. Blake's. That bespoke a man with a frightening temper. In fact, she had to wonder if Mr. Blake knew that his wife's shoes were in such sorry repair. If he didn't like to spend money, then he wouldn't want to replace the expensive silk shoes. Mrs. Blake might be frightened of him. When she'd covered her wrist at the theater, she'd certainly seemed wary of something.

Gabrielle returned before Rita did, with another armful of laundry. Katherine stepped aside, letting her into the room and trying not to get in her way. However, when she dumped these into the half-full basin, water splashed up and onto her hand. She hissed, clutching it close to her stomach and swearing under her breath.

Concerned, Harriet stepped forward and reached for Gabrielle's hand. "Are you hurt?"

Gabrielle grimaced. "It's a paper cut, nothing more." She held up her hand, and there was more than one paper cut between her thumb and index finger. The web of flesh looked permanently scarred with cuts that opened and closed and opened again.

"How did you get those?" They looked a good deal more painful than a common paper cut.

"It's no bother. I had to take over some of Ellie's tasks since she's been gone. I open the family correspondence now. Getting the seal open is ... problematic."

"Why don't you use an erasing knife?"

Gabrielle's shoulders slumped as she sighed. "I would, but I can't find the deuced thing. Wherever Ellie put it, it's gone. I don't dare ask Mr. Blake for another. If he won't replace her, he wouldn't replace a mere erasing knife."

The erasing knife Susanna used at home had a carved ivory handle, undoubtedly a fortune when one considered its purpose. If Mr. Blake's had been of the same quality, he would be incensed if asked to replace it. Gabrielle was probably afraid she would be blamed for losing it.

And why was the laundry maid tasked with opening the family correspondence? Shouldn't that have been handled by one of the upstairs maids? She opened her mouth to ask, but movement at the corner of her eye drew her attention to the doorway.

A small, pretty woman with an upturned nose and an armful of bedding paused on the threshold. "Oh. I didn't know we had guests..." Her voice trailed off and her eyes narrowed as she spotted Harriet.

She must be Rita. She was, Katherine acknowledged, remarkably pretty and delicate. Precisely the sort of woman a man like McTavish would leap to defend, under-estimating her. Katherine would make no such mistake.

Although they were in Mr. Blake's home and Rita had nowhere to run, Katherine sensed that the maid was mere heartbeats away from fleeing. She held up her hand, hoping to stop her. "Please, stay a moment. Harriet told me you are a friend of Ellie Simpson's. I only want to know what happened to her."

Muttering under her breath, Gabrielle chose that moment to escape. "I'll finish up upstairs." She slipped into the corridor and away.

Rita looked as though she would have dearly liked

to follow. Instead, one hand thrust into her apron pocket, she walked across the room and tossed the bedclothes into the basin. She didn't remove her hand when she used the stick to stamp them down.

Was she hiding something?

She didn't acknowledge Katherine at all. Katherine took that as a good sign, that Rita had not recognized who she was. Perhaps she had an opportunity to earn Rita's trust.

"It's simply dreadful how Bow Street is handling this. Saying they won't lift a finger to find her killer because she was a maid!"

A lie, but one that hit its mark. Rita raised her head, outraged or alarmed, Katherine couldn't tell.

She didn't answer, so Katherine carried on. "I knew Ellie. She spoke kindly of you all the time."

Rita hesitated. "How do you know who I am?"

"I recognized you from Ellie's descriptions. You are Rita, aren't you?"

Hesitantly, Rita nodded. "She..." Her voice warbled. She cleared her throat and started again. "She spoke kindly of me?"

She sounded surprised and perhaps even aggrieved.

Seeing that it was helping to open her up, Katherine lied. "She liked you a lot."

"She did?" Rita's voice was small.

"She did."

Pru added, "It's a shame, what happened. You must miss her."

Rita's face fell. She let the stick rattle to the ground and stuck both her hands in her apron pocket. "Yes, I do."

Pru leaned closer. Her voice a hush, she said, "I know she was a favorite of Mr. Blake."

Prudence Burwick, why would you say that?

The moment Rita's face darkened, Katherine feared that her attempts to gain the maid's trust had gone terribly awry. Her reaction was confirmation that she'd been jealous of Ellie, but it did little to prove that she was in fact Ellie's murderer.

Heedless of how far she was straying from Katherine's plan, Pru added, "It's odd... You informed Harriet you were at your mother's the night Ellie died. But I know you were here with her. Why would you lie?"

Rita stiffened. If Katherine and Pru hadn't been between her and the door, she undoubtedly would have run. "I didn't lie."

Abandoning her idea to earn the maid's trust, Katherine squared her shoulders and took charge of the interrogation. "You were seen with her that night."

"By who?"

"I won't name my source. But if you lied, we can only assume one thing."

Rita looked wary. "What?"

It was Harriet who hurled the accusation. "That you killed her. Or you know who did and you're covering for them."

"Killed her? No!"

Rita took a step back, bumping her calf against the basin and sloshing water over the far side. Katherine advanced on her, cornering her. "Tell us the truth. We know you have been having an affair with Mr. Blake. You were jealous of her, so you rid yourself of the competition."

Eyes wide, Rita glanced among the three of them. She found no allies. Her face was as pale as the linens in the water and nearly as transparent. "No. Why would I do that? He would only find someone else to take her place."

Katherine shrugged. "Perhaps you plan to kill them, too. Perhaps Ellie's betrayal was just that much worse because she was your friend. Either way, you will pay for your crimes today. You're coming with us to Bow Street, where they will beat a proper confession out of you if needed."

"You can't take me there!" Rita shouted, but she hunched her shoulders and pulled her left hand out of her pocket, throwing it in front of them like a shield. If Katherine really had meant to take her to Bow Street — which she had no authority to do — Rita made it even easier by providing her with the leverage to pull her out of the house.

She made no move to grab the woman, but she didn't back down. "We can, and we will. We have a friend there."

Rita swallowed hard. "Fine. I lied. But not because I killed her."

The confession rang in the empty room, accompanied only by the beating of Katherine's heart and the faint sound of her breaths. "If you didn't kill her, why did you lie?"

Rita wrung her hand in her apron, averting her gaze. She looked desperate. "She always acted so superior. Getting jewelry but keeping it a secret. Mr. Blake never gave me jewelry. So... when I saw her leave that night, I took advantage. I went into her room."

Harriet frowned. "You went into her room *after* she left? Gabrielle told me she heard you talking to her."

Rita tossed her hand in the air. "I might have been talking to myself, I don't recall. I was angry at her, at Mr. Blake, too. I only went in after she left because I didn't want her to see..."

"To see what?"

Katherine held her breath as she waited for an answer. After a moment's hesitation, Rita's posture turned defeated. She hung her head and reached deep into her pocket with her left hand. She pulled out both hands around a thin silver bracelet with a ruby clasp in the shape of a heart. "I took her bracelet. But I didn't kill her. I only lied about being at my mother's cottage because..." Her gaze darted toward Harriet. "I was afraid someone would discover that I stole the bracelet. It isn't the sort of thing a maid like me would have."

No, it wasn't. But more than that, Katherine was no longer concerned with the bracelet. She stared at Rita's right hand. Her pale hand was curled up and didn't grasp the silver band properly.

"Are you injured?"

Rita flushed scarlet. She mumbled under her breath, almost indecipherably. "My hand's been this way since birth. I can do my work just fine." She stuffed her misshapen and perhaps partially paralyzed hand into her pocket again. "Sometimes, Gabrielle helps me out and does the tasks that take two hands."

That explained why Gabrielle opened the mail, Katherine thought. Katherine's heart softened toward Rita. She had never seen a woman look so small, and it had nothing to do with Rita's stature. She was ashamed, and Katherine didn't think it was only because she'd been caught stealing. Tentatively, Katherine held up her hand, palm up. "If that was Ellie's, it should now go to her sister."

Mutely, Rita placed the bracelet in her hand.

"Are you going to tell her I was the one who took it?"

Katherine hesitated. Rita had been jealous, and she had done wrong, but she hadn't hurt anybody. With her right hand so paralyzed, she couldn't possibly be the killer. Wayland had been right, after all.

"I'll tell her I found it in the course of my investigation. She doesn't need to know anything else. But I must know, if you waited for Ellie to leave that night, can you tell me anything about what you might have seen? Did she seem agitated? Do you know anyone who would want to harm her?"

Still not meeting their gazes, Rita shook her head. "I only waited for her to leave. I wasn't paying much attention to how she seemed. But I don't know anyone who wanted to hurt her. It came as such a surprise." In a soft voice, she added, "Ellie was a nice girl. Better than me."

Katherine couldn't stand to see the tears gathering in the woman's face. But she didn't know this woman and couldn't offer her comfort. So instead, she beckoned to her companions and said, "Thank you for your time. I'll leave you to your chores."

Pru looked taken aback at the abrupt end to the conversation, but she didn't challenge Katherine until they stepped outside. Once the door was safely shut behind them, she complained, "She could have lied again. Those tears might have been false."

Katherine nodded. "They might have been, but Rita could not have killed Ellie."

As they mounted the stairs, Katherine couldn't see her friend's face, but the dubiousness in Pru's voice spoke for itself. "How can you know that?"

Katherine turned at the top to look the pair in the eyes. "It's simple. Lyle said the killer was right-handed. Rita would not have had enough strength in her right hand to stab a gnat, let alone a grown woman."

Harriet *tsk*ed under her breath. "Tarnation. I should have noticed that when we first met."

Katherine reached out, squeezing her maid's arm. "Don't worry about it, Harriet. It takes years to learn these things. And besides, Lyle only told us about the killer's right-handedness last night."

CHAPTER FOURTEEN

"This is dreadful!" Pru announced, her exclamation drowning out the rattle of the carriage wheels. Katherine winced at the exclamation, narrowing her eyes at Papa and Susanna as the carriage continued along. Susanna raised her eyebrows, pursing her lips.

"If you don't wish to come along, Miss Burwick, we would be happy to drop you at your fiancé's house along the way." The four of them were en route to Number Two Charles Street, where Lord Conyers was selling his townhouse.

Pru batted her hand through the air. "No, it's not that. It's our investigation."

Katherine shook her head tightly, but it was already too late.

Upon hearing about the investigation, Papa perked to attention. "Oh, has there been a new development?"

Katherine sighed. "Rather less of one. We were able to confirm yesterday that our primary suspect could not have committed the crime. She didn't have the strength."

Sagely, the earl nodded. He stroked his chin as if wondering whether to offer his advice. Although Katherine admired him, she didn't want to accept any advice that Wayland might later claim she used to cheat.

With a sigh, Pru mumbled, "I suppose Mrs. Blake is still a possibility, but she wouldn't have any need to be jealous, would she? Not with her own affair..."

Susanna pressed her lips together and turned to the shuttered window. "I'd rather not hear this."

She usually had more mettle than this, so Katherine had to wonder why she was being so squeamish over them speaking of the murder. Could it be the infidelity? Or perhaps it reminded her of the fact that her dear friend had been murdered only two months past. Katherine nodded solemnly. "Please, forgive us. We didn't mean to upset you."

Pru glared at her. Leaning closer, she whispered, "What if my Annandale is making more progress than we are? They haven't been following the same leads as us. And, even worse, they were right about our theory. We must find a better lead than them."

Katherine patted Pru's knee, trying not to let her friend's agitation affect her. Perhaps she ought to have collected Pru after this outing to the townhouse, when they were set to visit Sarah Simpson and deliver her sister's bracelet.

"Don't worry. What sort of things could they find out at the club, anyway? We will learn the same, if through a more circuitous route."

Pru lay back against the squabs again, but she didn't appear appeased. Darkly, she muttered, "It's unfair that women aren't allowed into clubs. But I suppose I'll wheedle any clues of my Annandale, in any case..."

The coach turned a corner and slowed to a stop. *Thank heavens*, Katherine thought with feeling. She exited the carriage at the first opportunity, thankful for the distraction.

The four-story, cheery yellow townhouse sold by Lord Conyers had a salacious past. He'd kept it as a trysting house, where he'd brought his lovers — including the victim of the murder that Katherine had investigated two months past. Although Katherine was a little bit leery of living in a house with such a scandalous past, the location was ideal.

Charles Street jutted off from St. James' Square, where a large park in the middle of the square provided the perfect romping place for Emma. It was near to Lord Annandale's house, where she could visit whenever they were in residence, and moreover, the price was right. She didn't want to spend all of her dowry on a house, the way she would if she were searching in Mayfair.

As they crossed the street and stepped up the swept stairs to the polished door, Pru jostled Katherine with her elbow. She pointed to the neighboring house, where the curtain rustled as the occupant hastily closed it. "At least you'll never have to worry about anyone breaking into your house. Mrs. Ramsey will certainly keep an eye on it when you're away."

So she had when Lord Conyers had owned it. Mrs. Ramsey, the neighbor, had been pivotal in providing the information Katherine had needed to solve the crime of Lord Conyers' dead lover. Having a busybody for a neighbor might prove advantageous — *if* Katherine liked the house. It wasn't as though she had been given a tour when last she'd been here, considering that she'd been investigating Lord Conyers for murder.

Since Mrs. Ramsey didn't seem inclined to brave the cold air, Katherine continued up the steps after her parents. A dour-faced man in a brown jacket and trousers opened the door and ushered them in.

The house itself was almost devoid of furniture. Katherine allowed her father and stepmother to lead as they toured each of the rooms, taking note of the structure of the house. It was smaller than the one Katherine currently occupied, which suited her greatly. For one thing, it would only be her, Emma, and Harriet here, perhaps with another new servant or two so Harriet didn't work herself to the bone. However, Katherine didn't require a house large enough to fit a family or even visitors, so this cozy edifice seemed perfect to her. It even had room for a separate library and study.

As Papa steered the solicitor into the kitchen for a private chat, Susanna turned to Katherine with an expectant look on her face. "Well? How do you like it?"

They stood in the least interesting of all the rooms, the front parlor with its dry hearth, brick mantel, and lonesome window facing out onto the snowy street. Katherine would much have preferred to be left to inspect the shelves taking up one of the upstairs rooms.

When she purchased the house, she would have plenty of time. Of all the places Susanna had searched out and recommended over the past several months,

Katherine liked this one best. It wasn't far from Pall Mall Street, where her Royal Society meetings were conducted. Not to mention, after such a long slog to find a house she liked, she would be happy to have it in her possession and be done with all this nonsense.

But there would be more technicalities to worry about next. She would need furniture, perhaps a footman strong enough to move it when needed, another maid, a cook... Or perhaps she would forego the cook and hire a housekeeper instead. They'd been given a tour of the servants' quarters as well, which seemed remarkably small, but perhaps if Harriet had a room to herself, she wouldn't much mind. Katherine had no idea how it compared to her room currently. Would it be too irregular for Katherine to give Harriet a room on the same floor where she slept?

"I like the house very much, I must admit."

Susanna beamed. "I do as well. It seems more than large enough for you, and best of all, it's nearby, so your father and I will be able to visit often."

Katherine hadn't considered that her parents would want to visit her. Perhaps she ought to hire a cook, after all...

The happy, expectant look on Susanna's face dimmed, and a furrow formed in her brow. She touched Katherine's arm lightly. "You do know that you're welcome to continue living with us. It is your home, too."

Katherine smiled, but shook her head. "Thank you, but I'm more than ready to live on my own. I think I'll like living here very much. But shouldn't I be involved in the price negotiations, not only Papa?"

Susanna shook her head curtly. "We know you're more than capable of taking care of such matters, but with the house's past, he might be able to finagle a better price from Lord Conyers. It's too sensitive a topic for the solicitor to speak to you about it directly, and you *are* an earl's daughter. You may as well take advantage of him."

Admittedly, Katherine would not have thought to haggle on the price based on what she knew of the house's past. "Whatever its history, I hear Lord Conyers has mended his unfaithful ways."

Susanna nodded. "I'd heard the very same thing, or near enough. His fiancée is insisting that he sell the townhouse if he wishes to move forward with the marriage. One of many reparations, as I understand it."

Pru shook her head. "The longer we investigate, the more it seems that all men stray from their wives into temptation. Have we investigated a case that didn't involve an affair by someone?"

At that moment, Papa stepped up close enough to

hear. He raised his eyebrows, solemn. "Most men are not like Lord Conyers. I assure you."

Susanna beamed over her shoulder at him. "I know, dear."

Katherine, too, nodded. She'd never known her father to stray from either of his wives. He was a loyal man, and other men had the same good character. However, they weren't usually the sort embroiled in murder investigations.

Pru hurried to answer. "Oh, I know my Annandale is not that sort of fellow."

Frowning, Susanna asked, "Then why do you delay so long in marrying him?"

Pru turned pink, turning her face away and mumbling. "I may not be delaying much longer."

"That's wonderful to hear, dear."

Since her friend seemed embarrassed at the attention, Katherine lifted her face to Papa's. "Is it all settled?"

Papa nodded. "He will relay my offer to Lord Conyers. I expect the answer to be favorable."

"And the sum? I trust it won't take the breadth of my dowry."

He laughed and patted Katherine on the shoulder. "I've only just awarded it to you. I'm not about to divest you of it. I negotiated a fair deal, perhaps even one in our favor. I gather the fellow is rather desperate for his fiancée not to toss him out with the refuse."

Having met Lord Conyers, Katherine had at first considered him incorrigible, until she'd learned the depth of his feeling for his dead mistress. He was capable of love. Perhaps, with time, he would find it for the wife he was set to marry for her fortune. The arrangement was one more reason why Katherine didn't care for marriage. It was more a business transaction to most than a matter of the heart.

Though, admittedly, that had never been true with her family.

The last to exit the house, Katherine shut the door behind her. Movement caught the corner of her eye, and she peered at Number Four Charles Street, where a figure rustled the curtain once more. She lifted her hand, waving to Mrs. Ramsey. With such an informative neighbor, Katherine would do well to maintain a good relationship with her.

By the time she reached the bottom of the steps, Mrs. Ramsey opened the door. A thin woman of middling height with thick, ash-blond ringlets and keen blue eyes, she pulled her shawl to cover her shoulders and throat. She frowned as her gaze brushed past the other four people and narrowed on Katherine. "You aren't looking for Lord Conyers, I hope."

Katherine shook her head. "Not this time. He's selling the house, and I'm hoping to buy it."

"Only you?"

Katherine nodded, firm. "Only me. Mrs. Ramsey, may I introduce you to my mother and father, Lord and Lady Dorchester? I believe you remember Miss Burwick?"

Mrs. Ramsey's mouth thinned, but after a moment she dropped into a curtsy. "It's nice to meet you, my lord, my lady." She settled her gaze on Katherine once more. "I must admit, I'm relieved to see that he is selling it. It was disturbing to see women coming in and out at all hours of the night. I hope you won't be doing anything similar?"

"She will not," Papa assured.

Mrs. Ramsey adjusted her shawl over her shoulders. When not frowning, she looked nearer to ten years Katherine's senior rather than fifteen. "Good. Not that I'm a busybody, or anything. I mean, I can keep my mouth shut. I'm not like some people, who might try to extort money to keep quiet about things I've seen. But I'd rather not have my neighbors gallivanting about with their sordid secrets."

Katherine's ears buzzed so loudly, she didn't hear Papa's response. Only days ago, he had warned her about how matters in the investigation might not always be as they seemed, and now Mrs. Ramsey's words had opened up another avenue of possibilities— ones that Katherine had not considered because she was expecting things to be *as they seemed.*

Mr. Blake did not give gifts to his wife, let alone the maids he took to bed. Yet Ellie had an expensive bracelet and a nightgown edged in expensive lace. Katherine had assumed those were *gifts* from Mr. Blake because they were having an affair.

Katherine had seen Mr. Blake associating with a man who, according to Wayland, liked to push the limits of the law.

Ellie had been caught stepping into Mr. Blake's carriage, something highly unlikely even if he was conducting an affair with her.

But what if he'd invited her into his carriage for another reason? Not to have an affair — but to quietly give her a payment. Perhaps Katherine had assumed the wrong motive all along! Ellie might not have been killed over jealousy at all — she may have been killed because she was blackmailing Mr. Blake!

CHAPTER FIFTEEN

Midmorning, shortly before noon, seemed the best time for Katherine and Pru to speak with Sarah Simpson. There was, logic dictated, a lull in the chores before the rush to make supper for the family. With that knowledge in mind, and wrapped in less expensive cloaks than they would usually have worn, the pair found themselves outside of the servants' entrance of Lady Lansing's house once more. Straightening her shoulders, Katherine rapped sharply on the door.

A sour-faced matron opened it, her expression turning even more bitter as she surveyed the two women on the doorstep. "Are you lost?"

Katherine must have done an admirable job of hiding her identity this time. Her smile faltered at the edges, but she carried on. "I know it's terribly inconvenient, but I must speak with Sarah. I have something to return to her."

For a moment, she feared that the matron would not step aside to let her pass. However, after glaring at both her and Pru in turn — a glare Pru matched — the woman stepped aside and spat two words.

"Five minutes."

From the authority in her voice, she must be the housekeeper, the woman to whom Sarah answered. The slight woman they sought stood at the counter, leisurely washing the breakfast dishes in a vat of mildly steaming water. She glanced up, brushing her cheek and leaving a wet smear. Her eyes widened as she recognized her visitors.

Unwilling to return the bracelet in full view of the housekeeper, Katherine asked, "Is there somewhere private we may talk?"

Sarah glanced at her superior for a long, hesitant moment before nodding. She dried her hands on her apron and gestured them forward. "We can speak in my room, if you don't mind using the stairs."

Katherine followed without hesitation.

If she'd known how many stairs were in the six-story townhouse, she might have reconsidered. By the time they reached the attic, her legs ached, but she refused to speak a word of complaint. Sarah led them down a corridor no wider than her shoulders to one of multiple plain white doors. She opened it into a room the size of Katherine's dressing room. What little space was there was eaten up by the narrow bed and basin of water. There wasn't a wardrobe, or a desk, or even a trunk to be found. The moment all three squeezed into the room, Sarah shut the door and turned to them.

"Have you discovered anything?"

"A little," Katherine answered. "We haven't yet made an arrest, but when Bow Street takes the person responsible into custody, I will make certain you are the first to know."

At the mention of the men whom Sarah believed to have done her sister wrong, she stiffened. Katherine didn't waste her breath reassuring the maid that her sister *would* be avenged. She knew Lyle would act once she found enough evidence. Justice would be served.

Before the aggrieved young woman sent them on their way, Katherine reached into her reticule and pulled out the silver bracelet. "In the meantime, I found this."

Sarah took it with trembling fingers. Reverently, she brushed her fingertips around the circlet before clutching it to her chest. Her eyes grew misty, and she sniffed. "Thank you. Where did you find it?"

"It was in Mr. Blake's house. They must have escaped his notice, or I'm certain it would have been returned to you."

Her chest rose swiftly as she sucked in an audible breath. "He won't accuse me of theft, will he?"

"It isn't theft. The bracelet is rightfully yours."

A happy smile pulled at Sarah's lips a moment before despondency overcame her once more. She looked down at the piece, brushing her finger over the ruby clasp. Her voice raw, she whispered, "Thank you. For bringing it back to me. I know she would have wanted me to keep it."

Her voice broke, and she turned away, squeezing between them and the bed before she stooped to pull a small box from beneath it. It was the same box she'd carried to the kitchen the day they had come to interview her. As she opened it, Katherine caught sight of the lace-edged nightgown.

"May I see that nightgown one more time?"

Sarah's expression grew shuttered. However, she didn't deny the request. Reluctantly, she pulled out the item. "Why do you want it?"

"I thought I felt some embroidery on it the first time I examined it."

Sarah nodded. She folded the garment inside out before pointing to a patch of needlework done in white, imperceptible against the muslin save for the raised ridges of the embroidery. Katherine traced her fingers over it. As she'd suspected the first time, it was a monogrammed M.

In the entirety of her investigation, she had yet to meet someone with the initial M. Was it insignificant? Her instincts clamored, telling her not to discount anything at this point. She still had a killer to find.

It seemed ludicrous for Ellie to have gone to the seamstress and ordered herself a nightgown with an embroidered M on the inside. However... if she had been receiving blackmail payments from Mr. Blake, could he have used this clothing as repayment? If true, he had either taken it from one of his mistresses — with an initial M — or had some association with the store where it had been made.

But without Ellie to question, or asking Mr. Blake, how were they to know where the garment had originated?

"Is it significant? Do you think this has anything to do with Ellie's murder?" Sarah asked.

Katherine wished she knew the answer to that question. "Everything is significant, but I don't have an answer for you yet. I promise you, we aren't about to stop searching. We *will* find who killed her sister. Even if we have to go back to the scene of the crime and work away from there."

Tears welled in Sarah's eyes, and she quickly stuffed the nightgown and the bracelet back into the box and out of sight. "See that you do. Ellie deserves better than she got. At the very least, she deserves justice."

CHAPTER SIXTEEN

At this midday hour, the streets were congested with sludge and carriages. Three blocks away from the crime scene, Katherine surrendered to frustration and bid the driver to stop and let them out. The moment she and Pru stepped foot into the damp snow, the cold leached through her boots and into her skin. She pulled her cloak closer around her and beckoned Pru forward with a wave of her hand.

At the first opportunity, she aimed to cut their walk shorter by means of an alley. Pru caught hold of her arm as she was about to step in.

"Are you certain we ought to be taking this route?"

Katherine frowned, looking down the deserted alley, the grayish snow marred with footsteps. When she glanced at her friend once more, the agitated expression on Pru's face clued her into her meaning.

"We won't meet Ellie's fate. For one, it's broad daylight, and we haven't a fire down the street to distract from any cries for help we make. For another, we haven't angered anyone enough that they would want to have us killed."

She raised her eyebrow to Pru, but her friend looked away as color formed twin spots in her cheeks. "Are you certain about that?"

The words were so low and mumbled that Katherine thought she might have misheard. She sighed and continued to trudge down the street instead. "Very well, we'll take the long way around. But Pru, we'll have to step foot in the same alley where she was killed. You know that, don't you?"

Although it had been six months since Ellie had been killed, and the rain and passage of time had washed away all evidence of the crime, Katherine still hoped to find some shred of inspiration from the crime scene.

Perhaps she was so deep in her thoughts that they were starting to manifest as reality, but as she passed a shop, she swore she saw that same stylized M that had been embroidered into the nightgown. She stumbled to a stop, turning to glance behind her.

Pru jumped, clearly still on edge from the idea of finding themselves in an alley alone. "What is it?"

Katherine took two steps back, still staring at the framed wooden sign hanging over a cheery yellow door. It swung in the stiff breeze, and the rain and sleet had weathered the paint until she thought she might be mistaken. But then, the sign fell flat, leaving its contents as plain as day: a stylized M, with a loop on the edge of one arm making it look like a sewing needle.

Katherine caught Pru's arm and pointed. "Do you recognize that?"

Pru squinted but shook her head.

"I suppose it's different if you're looking at it rather than feeling it. I'm certain this is the same sigil I found embroidered into Ellie Simpson's nightgown."

"It is?" Pru stepped closer and craned her neck to look. "I suppose it might be. Let's go inside and find out."

Katherine concurred. The crime scene had waited six months; it could wait a few more minutes while they followed this new potential lead.

The door stuck a bit as she shouldered it open. The breeze followed them as they stepped inside, rustling a rack of ribbons. After they shut the door, the ribbons quieted and went still, leaving them in a paradise of fabrics. Perhaps Katherine ought to have guessed from the needle worked into the emblem.

Although Katherine and Pru both frequented modistes in London, they usually did so near Bond Street, rather than a small nondescript tailor in the middle of this neighborhood. It bordered the gentrification, but also catered to the working class — the Hound and Ale Pub, especially.

Yet Katherine's expert eye picked out fabrics that would not have been out of place on a duchess. The brilliant, jewel-bright silks that ran over one table, drawing the eye, almost seemed to mute the bolts of lace on the smaller table next to it. Near the ribbon rack were other tables, embroidery thread in delicate silk colors to match, carefully sculpted ivory buttons in matched sets, wickedly sharp shears in sizes ranging from the length of Katherine's forearm to the length of her pinky finger, stylized silver thimbles, and little delicate embellishments meant to be sewn into necklines and hems. Beyond these were a display of ready-made silk shirts and dresses. Who in this neighborhood could afford a modiste like this?

Katherine and Pru exchanged a glance, their eyebrows raised. Katherine stepped forward first, careful where she placed her feet lest she track in the sludge from the street. She stopped next to a bolt of indigo cloth that reminded her of a peacock.

"Ah, I see you have found my new shipment."

The woman's voice was heavily accented with French. If Katherine had not spoken French, she might have mistaken it for a Parisian accent. However, the vowels contained far too much good English for the speaker to have been native to France. Clearly, the woman didn't know the difference, to be putting on a fake accent.

Katherine trailed her fingers over the silk as she turned to look at the fraud. The shopkeeper was a short woman, the affluence of her store evident in her rounded hips and face. Was it that horrid accent that gave her customers confidence in her?

She gestured with both hands to the table, a delicate movement. "They just arrived from *belle Paris*." She pronounced the city name in the French style, rolling the R as she exaggerated the word.

Beau Paris, Katherine inwardly corrected. Paris was not a feminine word in French.

Although the origin of the shopkeeper was in question, the origin of the fabric was less so. They might well have been imported from France, but at what cost? Curious, Katherine ran her hand over the nearest bolt of silk, but she couldn't tell the difference between this and the real thing. If it was fraudulent, she couldn't tell.

"Is that the only thing you've gotten from Paris recently?"

The smile on the woman's face broadened. She gestured to the table. "The lace as well, of course. If it all meets your fancy, *madame*, perhaps I can show you some fashion plates I had sent at the same time. You'll be the most stylish *madame* this side of Dover."

Katherine removed her hand from the fabric and turned to face the woman directly. "The lace you have is very fine. I suppose you sell a lot of it. I'm sorry, I've never seen this shop before, are you the owner?"

"Just so, *madame*. *Oui, oui!* I am Madame Manteau."

Mrs. Coat? She certainly must not cater to any sort of educated clientele. *Manteau* was a common enough word that someone with a cursory knowledge of French ought to have learned it.

"Come this way. I'll show you everything I can do with this lace. I don't long have it in the store before it is gone."

Unless her prices matched those of the other stores Katherine had found herself in — and unless she was catering to the circle of lords and ladies to which Katherine belonged, she thought not — she certainly believed it. Lace was a rare commodity, especially for those who didn't have a fortune to spend upon it.

"A friend of mine had a nightgown that I believe was made by you. Do you always embroider your signature into the garment?"

"Ah, well, I must make my mark." The woman laughed, a deep, hearty sound. "How else will people know where to buy their next triumph?"

Katherine remained silent on the subject.

Pru took up the interrogation where Katherine left off. "Perhaps you remember our friend, then. She was about as tall as you, but thinner and with blond hair." Pru continued to describe Sarah Simpson, and if she and Ellie were indeed identical twins, the description ought to spark some sort of memory with this woman.

Madame Manteau pursed her vibrantly painted lips. She shook her head. "I'm afraid I don't recall. A woman like this, I see many of them in a week."

With all the delicate work that needed to be done in order to produce that nightgown, Katherine doubted she'd forgotten such an important client. All of the modistes whom Katherine had worked with could have named their client list from memory. Often they did, bragging in order to induce their customers to spend even more at a fitting in order to outdo their rivals. That rivalry, and the recommendation of their clients to their friends, was how modistes typically made their fortune.

However, Madame Manteau had set herself apart as an entirely different sort of seamstress from her very first words.

"Do men often buy nightgowns for their mistresses, perhaps?" Katherine asked.

Madame Manteau gasped. "For their *wives*, you mean? I'm certain none of my clients would be so scandalous as to dally with a woman to whom they are not married."

Oh, please. Katherine bit back a sigh.

Perhaps Mr. Blake had lied and told the woman he wished the nightgown made for his wife. It would be irregular for the seamstress not to meet her client and take her measurements, but considering the clothes on display in the store, Katherine decided it *might* be possible.

Or she might be wasting her time. In any case, if someone with as deep pockets as Mr. Blake had stepped foot in this store, Madame Manteau would certainly have taken note of it.

"Oh yes, of course. Slip of the tongue. I don't suppose Mr. Blake, an import merchant, ever purchased such a nightgown from here? It's made of muslin and has lace edging. I rather liked it."

"Who? I'm sure I don't know this gentleman you tell me of."

So she said, but her accent slipped, and she blinked rapidly as she spoke. The moment the sentence slipped off her tongue, she was gesturing to the table again, her persona in place again. "If you want, I can make this garment for you. All you need to do is choose the pattern of lace you like, yes?"

"You don't know Mr. Blake?"

"I'm sure even if I did, I would not be able to tell you something so personal about my client. I do not disclose the sort of things that my clients wish me to make. It would be bad for business."

Her eyes snapped, as final a warning as her tone.

Katherine pressed her lips together to hide her disapproval.

"Perhaps you recall the time of year, then," Pru added. "Surely you remember the night of the fire, when the Hound and Ale Pub burned down? I believe the item was purchased near then."

Propping her hands on her hips, Madame Manteau shook her head so vigorously a lock of hair fell to curl around her cheek. "I'm sure it cannot be. I was not here that night. I only heard about it in the morning. I was so relieved to see that my shop was unharmed."

From her look of affront and high color, Katherine couldn't tell whether she was flustered by the question or by the memory.

"You want this nightgown? I have a few set designs I do. I can pull out the plates to show you."

"No. If you don't recall, that won't be necessary. Thank you for your time."

Katherine wasn't interested in purchasing from the shop, but she was disappointed that she hadn't learned more.

"Come, Pru."

Her footsteps weighed with reluctance, Pru followed as Katherine left the shop. Once the door was wedged shut behind them, Katherine turned to her friend.

"Do you think she was lying?"

"About being at the shop on the night of the fire?"

Katherine pressed her lips together, humming under her breath as she steered Pru down the street toward their original destination. "Perhaps, but I was thinking more about Mr. Blake. Did you notice the way her accent slipped when I asked about him? And she seemed defensive."

Slowly, Pru nodded. "But you can't think he went into a shop like that and bought a lace-edged nightgown for Ellie. It's the sort of thing he would give a lover, and wouldn't he have servants to do errands like that?"

"But if she was blackmailing him, he might not have wanted anyone to know."

Pru cocked her head to the side. "Why would she ask for a nightgown and not for money?"

Katherine sighed. Could it simply be because Ellie would never be able to afford such a garment? Unfortunately, Katherine might never know for certain. "That seems to be the question, doesn't it? Perhaps if we visit the scene of the crime, we will be able to think of something more."

If nothing else, the walk would help to clear her head.

CHAPTER SEVENTEEN

As expected, the scene of the crime held no clues. It was a wide alley, big enough for Katherine and Pru to walk abreast. But despite some stained bricks and refuse she'd rather not think about, it held no clue as to who might have killed Ellie Simpson.

She hadn't expected it to, but Katherine couldn't help the twinge of disappointment nevertheless. She had hoped standing in the scene of the crime would have inspired some latent idea that would propel her to solving the case. Unfortunately, all that littered the alley was blustery snow and cold air.

"This is closer to the Hound and Ale Pub than I thought it would be."

Katherine glanced up at Pru's voice. "We knew it

was nearby. After all, if it had been too far, the fire would not have held everyone's attention."

Impatient, Pru huffed. "Yes, I know that. But isn't that the pub just around the corner? If so many people were milling about, how did they fail to notice Ellie's plight?"

"At my best guess, no one notices a maid. If she had been of higher birth, her situation might have bestirred the crowd a bit more."

Pru didn't look happy with the answer. If Katherine were honest, she wasn't happy to give it.

However, the reminder about the fire stirred something in the back of Katherine's mind. She searched the alley for signs of scorch marks, smoke stains on the walls, but found nothing. However, her examination brought to her mind's eye the last thing that had been burned.

"Mr. Blake's boots."

Pru looked at Katherine oddly. "I know you like to curse, but that's a bizarre one even for you."

Katherine laughed. She couldn't help herself. "No, Mr. Blake's boots were burned. Remember? Harriet's friend was trying to fix them and bemoaning that she never could. Maybe Mr. Blake was out here the night of the fire."

Pru looked dubious. "But Ellie was killed before

the rain and, therefore, before the fire. Plus, the fire didn't spread to the alley. He wouldn't have gotten his boots burned if he was in the alley doing away with Ellie."

Tarnation. Katherine bit the edge of her tongue as she tried to think of an explanation. "Perhaps after he killed Ellie, he tried to blend with the crowd that had gathered around the fire. He would have been able to disappear among them and look as though he had valid cause to be there."

Pru raised her eyebrows. "Didn't you just say that someone with as auspicious a lineage as Mr. Blake would have been remarked upon that day?"

She had, hadn't she? Katherine bit the inside of her cheek, but she shook her head nonetheless. "I suppose it's possible, but Mr. Blake isn't an earl. He isn't a duke or a viscount or even an honorary lord. He's a mere mister, if a wealthy one."

"People see wealth, don't they?"

That they did. And yet, no one had told the authorities that they had seen Mr. Blake that night.

Or perhaps the officers of Bow Street simply hadn't asked, due to the fire.

"You're right. There are few shops around here. If the owners were in, perhaps they would have seen Mr.

Blake, or someone, with a woman of Ellie's description. Let's ask."

Eager to be out of the alley, Pru led the way to the street. The first shop they entered was that of a chandler. His candles smelled strongly of tallow, and Katherine suspected that he didn't have anything fine enough to be seen in her father's house. Nevertheless, she tried not to wrinkle her nose and caught the eye of the aging shopkeeper.

"I have a bit of a bizarre request for you, sir."

His bushy eyebrows pulled together, but he seemed amenable enough. He nodded, gesturing for her to continue. "I'll see if I can please, milady. Though I warn, if it doesn't have to do with candles, I'm not your man."

The tables with their wares reached up to her elbows, propelling her down the narrow aisle to the counter where he now rested.

"I'm wondering about the evening the Hound and Ale burned down. Were you in the shop that day?"

The shopkeeper shook his head. "There was a frightful storm. No one comes in for candles during a storm. I closed up and went home to my bed. I'm lucky the fire didn't spread to me."

So he was. Dejected, Katherine thanked him and led Pru out of the shop.

The next shop they entered belonged to that of a milliner. Pru took the lead this time, and Katherine relinquished the interview to her. Although brusque, Pru usually asked the right questions. Not to mention, she was far better at convincing the owner, a thin woman with gray threading her hair, that she was not at all interested in buying a new hat or gloves.

"Were you open the day the Hound and Ale burned?"

The woman gasped. "Yes I was, and I nearly got burned along with her! If not for the fire brigade, those flames would surely have taken my entire shop."

"You must have been terrified," Katherine said to soften Pru's approach.

The shopkeeper nodded, clasping her hands in front of her stomach.

"This may seem odd, but we are trying to locate Mr. Blake and his whereabouts that night. You might recall him, he's the fellow who carries around the crest of a wineglass in front of a barrel."

The woman's eyes widened, but to Katherine's astonishment, she nodded. Katherine's heart lodged in her throat. She held her breath, waiting for the woman's next words.

"Well, he must have been there. It was pandemonium, and I... I didn't see him directly. But I do recall seeing his carriage up on Young Street. You see, I keep my grandson up there with a friend while I work during the day. The moment the fire struck, I ran to retrieve him, and I'm certain I saw his carriage — Mr. Blake's, that is, not my grandson." The woman gave a delicate laugh that Katherine barely even heard.

"Thank you. You've been very helpful."

"Are you sure I can't interest you in a pair of new gloves? It's terribly cold outside."

Pru declined in a way that left little room for argument. When she turned toward the door, Katherine followed, her ears ringing. Young Street. That was four blocks north of where they now stood. Only four blocks north of the fire, two blocks north of the scene of Ellie's murder.

The moment they stepped foot in the street once more, Pru turned to her with bright eyes. "That's what we need, isn't it? The proof that Mr. Blake was here that night."

As much as Katherine wanted to say yes, she hesitated. "It's proof that his carriage was here. He might have been in the Hound and Ale Pub when it caught fire... He might have been strolling past. Or perhaps it was Ellie who had taken that carriage and left it so far from the crime scene."

Pru frowned. "Why was Ellie here in the first place? This is far from the Blake household."

That it was. Why had Katherine not asked herself that question yet? "The only explanation I can think of at the moment is that she came here to collect her blackmail payment. That would have been why Mr. Blake was here as well, don't you think?"

"We must confirm with another source. If the carriage was here, so was Mr. Blake's driver. We must speak with him."

Pru smiled. "We have some time before we have to meet the men at the meeting tonight. Why don't we go now?"

KATHERINE STUMBLED into a deep puddle near the livery where Mr. Blake stabled his horses. The icy sludge wet her shoes just above the soles, creating an ugly waterline on the sides. She cursed under her breath and shook out the wet soles, thanking her good luck that the water had not sloshed on the tops, where the soiling would be more visible. And the fact that she'd decided to wear sensible shoes today.

Since she was going to see Mr. Blake's driver, she elected to pretend to be in the market for a carriage.

She'd used this excuse once before during an investigation. It seemed not having one's own carriage yet came in handy. To that effect, she and Pru had left her father's carriage several blocks behind and walked the rest of the way. After this near soaking, Katherine couldn't help but wonder if she should buy a carriage in truth. After all, once she moved to Charles Street, she would no longer have the use of her father's coach.

Regardless of her sincerity, the excuse granted her and Pru entrance into the livery that served the entire street. After that, it wasn't difficult to discover who Mr. Blake's driver was. The driver, too, wore livery emblazoned with the crest Mr. Blake had awarded himself. For a man who didn't like to spend money, he certainly enjoyed advertising its presence.

Although he was easy to find, Mr. Blake's driver was close-lipped. He gave short answers as Katherine asked a variety of questions about the carriage, including its comfort and ease of use.

Katherine wouldn't have expected him to have any kind of loyalty to Mr. Blake. After all, if Mr. Blake wouldn't hire another maid to replace one who had died, what scraps would he be likely to give his driver? So, after warming him up a bit with the mundane questions, she asked the questions she'd really come to find the answer about.

"This may seem irregular, but I heard a most curious rumor."

The man stiffened. Belatedly, Katherine recalled his rumored dalliance with Mrs. Blake. She didn't dare ask about that, as there was no way he would tell the truth. She hurried on before he gave them the cut direct.

"I wonder if you might confirm it for me. A friend of mine said that she saw Ellie Simpson using Mr. Blake's carriage."

The driver scowled. "A maid, in the carriage? Is your friend blind? Of course she wasn't using the carriage for her own means. The maids aren't even allowed to use the carriage for errands. *If* there's nothing else..."

Katherine stepped to the side to bar him from leaving. "Are you certain? My source was adamant."

He scowled. "It's been a right long time since she would have used one of the rigs, in any case. Haven't you heard the lady in question is dead?"

"I have. This report, admittedly, is from six months ago."

Grumbling, the man looked as though he wished for an escape between her and Pru. For once, Pru's solid figure worked to their advantage as they hemmed him in. "It's important we find out. We can be very close lipped—even on rumors about certain ladies and their drivers if they've helped us with information."

Darn Pru! Why did she threaten him with that? But apparently it worked. His eyes narrowed, and he thought for a few beats then nodded.

"I suppose she might have stepped inside for a minute. But no more than that. And if you've heard rumors about her, you've certainly heard rumors about my employer."

Obviously, the driver often paused to let women into the carriage with Mr. Blake. How many dalliances could one man have? Perhaps it was better that she didn't know! She only cared about one particular woman.

"And would that have happened near the Hound and Ale Pub the day it burned down? I understand Ellie was in the area at the time."

"Of course not," the man spat. "I did not drive Mr. Blake down to that area of town. I was nowhere near the fire, and I was glad to be out of it — it was the worst storm of the season! Perhaps a woman like yourself wouldn't know it, but a man like me would have been stuck on the outside seat with the horses."

Katherine bristled at the insult in his tone.

Unwilling to remain with them despite their

efforts, the prickly man glowered at them both. "I have duties to be about, if you'll excuse me, ladies."

As dearly as Katherine would have loved to continue questioning him, she stepped aside and let him pass. He seemed on the edge of making a scene, not caring that he was in the presence of an earl's daughter. She sighed as he hurried back to his task and braced herself to step out into the cold once more.

"At least we can be certain that Ellie was black-mailing Mr. Blake."

Katherine glanced sidelong at her friend. "What makes you say that?"

Pru raised her eyebrows. "There's only one reason a woman would get in the carriage for only a few minutes. I doubt even Mr. Blake is quick enough to tryst in that short a time span."

Maybe she was right. Katherine had little idea of how such things worked, but apparently Pru had been researching for her impending marriage. Katherine laughed. "Well, that's hardly proof, but I would say it supports our idea of the blackmail in addition to the bracelet and fancy garment, but we have no proof that he was near the scene of the crime, and the driver seems very reluctant to admit it. We'll need to look harder."

Pru sighed, but she didn't object. "I'm sure he was

lying about that. But it seems odd. Why tell us that Ellie stepped into the carriage for only a moment but then deny the day?"

"Good question." As she turned to step away, Katherine clasped her elbow. "Don't you dare tell any of this to Lord Annandale. We are so close to solving this case, I can taste our triumph. I don't want him and Wayland to gain the upper hand."

Pru glared and pulled away. "What sort of ninny do you take me for? I assure you, not a word of this will leave my mouth."

Katherine smiled. "Good. Because all we need is one more piece of solid evidence before we can prove our case."

CHAPTER EIGHTEEN

B y the time Katherine reached Pall Mall Street, the meeting was in full swing. She and Pru stepped lightly up the old, creaking steps to the bubble of conversation spilling from the upper floor. As they reached the designated meeting area, a large room flanked in one corner by comfortable armchairs and in the other corner by a long table with utilitarian seating arrangements, the room was filled to the brim with detectives and investigation enthusiasts. Katherine steeled herself for the ordeal to come. At some point tonight, Wayland would undoubtedly attempt to learn everything she had discovered today.

In fact, her eyes gravitated to the gentleman in question. Or perhaps it was simply that he was so tall, the eye naturally fell on his person.

If that was the case, then clearly Katherine suffered from the same affliction. Because the moment she spotted him in the crowd, he turned from his conversation with a shorter fellow and pinned her with a stare too distant for her to decipher. Katherine swallowed hard and tried to rein in her trepidation. Tonight, Katherine would have to admit that Wayland had been right about her suspicions regarding her theory. And, if luck was not on her side, he might already be pursuing a more fruitful avenue. Had he solved the case already? She was so close to victory...

"There he is!"

Pru pointed across the room to a different man, her fiancé. As she lifted her hand in a wave, calling him closer, a broad grin split his face and seemed to light the air more brightly than the candles scattered around in sconces. He excused himself from his conversation and loped toward them.

Lord Annandale and Wayland reached them at the same time. The moment they did, Lord Annandale lifted his fiancée's hand and pressed a kiss to her palm. "It's been a right trying day without you."

She blushed prettily. "Mine, too. The company hasn't been the same."

Katherine raised her eyebrows and pinned her friend with a dubious stare. Pru didn't even seem to notice her displeasure, she was so enraptured by her fiancé's presence.

Wayland smirked. He motioned with his chin to a free area near to the door and whispered, "Perhaps we ought to leave them to their reunion."

Katherine made a face. "They've been apart little more than a day."

His gaze twinkled. "So you think."

She raised her eyebrows. "Do you know something I don't?"

His grin widened, and they fell into step as he led her toward that secluded spot. "I always do."

Katherine snorted. "Oh? Is that why you're always cajoling me for information?"

"Perhaps I like the sound of your voice."

Katherine fought the urge to roll her eyes. "Don't flatter me."

He laughed. "Very well. Call me curious. How did your theory regarding Mr. Blake's maid turn out?"

Rita. Katherine bit her lip to hold in a sigh. She didn't want to admit that she was wrong, but she could see no way of neatly sidestepping the question.

Especially not when Wayland raised both eyebrows and pinned her with a knowing glance. "Did you find proof that she killed Ellie Simpson?"

"I'm working on another theory." Katherine bit off her words, struggling not to scowl.

Wayland laughed. She hadn't fooled him one bit.

Her scowl deepening, she glared at him. "And how has *your* idea played out, pray tell?"

Unfortunately, he wasn't perturbed by the question. He widened his smile and answered, "We are working on it." He raised his gaze and his hand toward the door. "I see they're through with their reunion."

When he strode off, it was the fastest Katherine had ever seen him retreat.

"I should learn the trick to doing that so I can repeat it."

She hadn't meant the words for anyone but herself. However, upon reaching her, Pru must have heard. With a quizzical look, her friend asked, "What was that?"

Katherine shook her head. "Nothing. I was woolgathering. Are you sure you want to part ways with Lord Annandale so soon?"

"Actually..." Pru nibbled on her lip, the color rising in her cheeks as she glanced back toward her future husband. "I think he and Wayland are very close to working out another clue. Perhaps even tonight. We ought to stick near them, so we don't miss anything. I'm happy to watch my Annandale, of course, but..."

Katherine sighed. "I'll stay near to Wayland, then. For the good of the investigation," she added, in case Pru was wont to get any ideas.

"You'd best hurry to catch him then, because I think he's trying to catch someone's eye."

That devil, he was! Katherine hitched her skirts and hurried through the gathered crowd. Wayland was striding with purpose toward the table on the far end, where a ring of detectives listened as Lyle gave a demonstration of one of his latest inventions. Katherine gave him a little wave a moment before she caught up with Wayland.

As she stepped into place at his side, he peered down at her with a frown. Granted, she didn't enjoy his teasing, but he could appear less displeased to have her nearby.

It soured her mood, but she tried not to show it with so many eyes taking note of them. "I hope you don't mind if I keep you company. It seems Pru craves a few more moments alone with her fiancé."

Helpless, Wayland looked over his shoulder as if seeking confirmation. By then, Pru had latched herself onto Annandale. The pair looked as though they didn't notice the rest of the room existed. With a beleaguered smile, Wayland offered her an arm. "I was just taking a tour of the room to stretch my legs. Will you accompany me?"

The moment she acquiesced and slipped her palm onto his arm, he steered her away from the table. She glanced over her shoulder, trying to catalogue the members there. Which had he hoped to speak with? Come to think of it, whom had he interrupted his conversation with when she'd arrived?

He couldn't be waiting for Lyle, could he? Lyle had promised her to be neutral in this matter, and she trusted him wholeheartedly. If he had something of import to impart regarding the investigation, he would divulge it to her as well as Wayland. Yet someone near here must have drawn his attention...

As Wayland led her toward the chairs on the far side, a man straightened from the table with a wave. Katherine licked her lower lip as she tried to recall his name. Mr. Pell, wasn't it? He wasn't assigned to Bow Street but worked for one of the less auspicious detective agencies in town. The sort that investigated infidelities among spouses. In so banal a workplace, Mr. Pell hadn't yet gained prominence in the Society. However, from crossing paths with him once or twice before at meetings, Katherine knew him to have a sound head on his shoulders.

But why would Wayland be discussing the case

with him? Perhaps she wasn't reading into the situation correctly.

When she turned to face forward once more, she caught Wayland looking over his shoulder with a pained expression. He changed their trajectory again, this time leading them towards the door as if he meant to leave.

"Captain Way—"

Wayland quickened his stride, but Katherine dug in her heels. "What's the rush? You'll have me tripping over my heels if you don't slow down."

He raised an eyebrow at her as if he didn't believe her flimsy excuse for a second.

She met him with an identical expression. "I have a reputation for clumsiness, or have you forgotten?"

He made a choked sound that sounded suspiciously like a snort before he turned away. He picked at the cravat at his throat. "It's hot in here. I need some air. If you're so desperate to keep my company..."

"Not desperate," Katherine protested.

An air of smugness wrapped around him like a cloak. "In that case, perhaps you won't mind if I step out for a moment and return to collect you later."

She most certainly would mind. She was not a stray puppy. She would have told him, if Mr. Pell had not crossed within earshot at that very moment.

Instead, she directed her attention toward him. "Ah, Mr. Pell, I didn't see you there. Were you looking for Wayland?"

Wayland cast her a nervous glance, as if wondering at her sweet tone.

A moment later, his nonchalant air was back in place. Almost bored, he said, "Oh, I'm sure it's nothing important. He wishes to talk about war stories, don't you, Mr. Pell? I wouldn't want to tire your delicate ears, Lady Katherine."

Katherine sent him a barbed smile. "Oh no, I insist. Please, tell your stories."

Mr. Pell looked dumbfounded. He glanced from Wayland to Katherine and back again, as if uncertain what to say. Clearing his throat, he straightened his collar and suggested, "Er, weren't you about to tell me the one about... Spain?"

Captain Wayland, to Katherine's knowledge, had not been positioned in Spain.

She leaned forward, feathering her hand over Mr. Pell's sleeve. "You can speak plainly, sir. I'm involved in the same investigation as Wayland. If you don't tell me now, he'll only share the information with me later." She offered Wayland another of her saccharine smiles.

He did not look amused.

Mr. Pell, on the other hand, took her at her word. After a surreptitious glance to check that no one nearby was paying them any mind, he turned his full focus on her. Everyone was engrossed in their own conversations, these being meetings of the minds, where ideas were exchanged in great volume.

With a brief moment of hesitation, he studied Wayland. In a hushed voice, the detective informed, "I discovered the warehouse you were looking for. Mr. Blake lets one a mere two buildings away from the pub that burned this summer, the Hound and Ale. Rumor has it that he stores his smuggled silk and lace in there before he turns them over to local businesses to legitimize them."

Katherine raised her eyebrows. Mr. Blake, a smuggler? She thought he had made his fortune in wine, not in silk. "Please, go on. Did you learn anything more?"

Wayland glared at the man as if demanding silently that he cease his report at once. Unfortunately for him, Mr. Pell had set his attention on Katherine. The detective was a plain-looking man not more than thirty, and he seemed rather enthusiastic to show his abilities to her.

"I've been watching the warehouse all week. I watched Mr. Blake come with Lord Quinbury. They both got out of Quinbury's carriage — it's a wonder he can even afford that carriage."

"Oh?"

Mr. Pell shook his head, looking disgusted. "Rumor has it Quinbury has gambled away his family's fortune. Men like that don't deserve money. In any case, he wants to join in on Mr. Blake's smuggling business to replenish his coffers. I asked around. Their association dates back several months. In fact, the two of them were ensconced in the warehouse the afternoon the Hound and Ale went up in flames. They must have a secret cellar or something, because I have it on good account that they didn't notice the fire until *after* they concluded their game of loo. Quinbury's carriage had been outside for hours, and he lost half his fortune to Blake, what remained of it. Since they're still amiable, I imagine he must have decided to go into business with Blake, after all."

Katherine's stomach sank as her sole suspect slipped out of her grasp. "No, you must be mistaken. Mr. Blake couldn't have been with Lord Quinbury on the afternoon the Hound and Ale burned." Was Quinbury a reliable alibi, though? He was an unsavory character and could have lied for Blake. But something about Blake setting up a card game so he could slip out and kill Ellie didn't seem right. If that were the case, then it meant Ellie hadn't come to the area with Blake, and if that was true, then *why* was she there, so far from home?

Mr. Pell pressed his hand over his heart. "I assure you, my lady, I am the picture of thoroughness when it comes to these matters. I checked several sources and had them confirm, including Lord Quinbury's valet. The man was turned out the next day. Quinbury had lost the money to pay the fellow!"

Katherine didn't know how to answer, considering that her entire investigation was crumbling in front of her eyes. However, Mr. Pell looked so expectant that she couldn't help but give him a small smile of encouragement. "My word, that is thorough. Have you worked on many cases with Captain Wayland?"

The fellow shrugged. "A few. He has work for me from time to time. I hear you're also involved in the investigation business, my lady. If you come across any work that's too dirty for your delicate hands, be sure to pass it my way."

He dug into his pocket and took out a smudged card, handing it over with his details. When she reached for it, his fingers curled around her hand, and he held her in place, his eyes locked with hers. "Feel free to send me a message. For anything you might need."

She mustered a smile and tucked the card into her reticule without looking at it. "Of course."

When she glanced up at Wayland, she found him scowling at Mr. Pell with a thunderous look. Good grief! He couldn't be so cross with the fellow for spilling the information, could he? After all, it hadn't helped Katherine in the least. Her only suspect was now up in the air!

At least the information was not a total loss. If the Duke of Quinbury had not only lost his fortune but gotten involved with illegal activities like smuggling... Perhaps she had another reason for Miss Graylocke not to marry him. She could rest easy knowing that she had accomplished one of her goals, even if it was the far less important one. But how could she make Miss Graylocke's parents aware of that? She couldn't possibly tell them she'd stumbled upon the information while investigating an old murder. She'd have to think of something else.

Mr. Pell hurried to excuse himself and slip back into the crowd when Wayland's expression did not lighten. The moment he was away, Katherine patted Wayland on the arm and said, "Perhaps you ought to get that air now. You look like you have a headache."

She turned on her heel and searched out her friend before he had time to quip a response.

She caught Pru's eye before she'd taken two steps. Within moments, Pru separated herself from her fiancé. She met Katherine midway. The moment she did, she latched onto Katherine's elbow and pulled her to the side of the room. "I saw you talking to someone with Wayland. What did you learn?"

Katherine grimaced. "Mr. Blake could not have killed Ellie. He was with Lord Quinbury that afternoon, playing loo. And it seems both he and Quinbury are up to their eyeballs in smuggling."

"Smuggling?"

"Yes. Silk and fine lace like the garment that Ellie had. There has to be some connection, but if Lord Blake was with Quinbury, how could he have murdered Ellie?"

Pru seemed deep in thought, so Katherine let her gaze wander. Rather than lightening her mood, the exchange of information around her was claustrophobic. Perhaps she was the one who ought to get some air. Or perhaps, weary as she was, she would go home for the evening instead.

As she set about doing that very thing, promising Pru that they would meet the next day to go over the clues with Harriet, she spotted another esteemed friend. The Duchess of Tenwick, Philomena.

At last, Katherine realized how she would pass

along the information she'd gathered about Miss Gray-locke's ill-fated groom. With her connection to the family, Philomena could pass the news along. And while she was at it, Katherine would have Phil put in a good word for Lord Glendore, as well. Miss Graylocke deserved to have the marriage of her heart.

CHAPTER NINETEEN

The next day, having finished informing Pru and Harriet about the clues she had learned last night at the Royal Society meeting, Katherine leaned back in the drawing room chair and ran her fingers over Emma's fur. The dog wriggled in her lap in glee, turning over onto her back to offer her belly. Silence dominated the room as everyone absorbed the information. Katherine could practically hear the ticking of their thoughts in time to the grandfather clock as they pieced together what they had discovered about the murder investigation and tried to fit in the missing piece.

"If Mr. Blake went straight from the game of loo at his warehouse to the fire next door, he cannot be a killer. His warehouse is south of the crime scene, with the Hound and Ale between them."

It was a fact Katherine had mulled over in her head hour after hour last night, lamenting the loss of her latest suspect.

Crossly, Pru said, "We should verify that he was in fact at that card game. Do you think that's why his driver lied about being there the night of the fire?"

"No, I think they were in Quinbury's carriage that night, so Blake's driver told the truth. Though I sure thought he was lying, and didn't one of the shop owners say she saw Blake's carriage four blocks north of the fire?" Katherine said.

"Maybe Blake let Ellie take it as part of their blackmail deal because Ellie wanted to shop in the finer stores?" Pru suggested. "The driver might have seen that as a reason to lie."

Katherine sighed. When her fingers stilled, Emma whined. Idly, Katherine soothed herself with the touch of Emma's soft fur. "We can look for Lord Quinbury's former valet and verify if Blake was in his carriage, but Mr. Pell has no incentive to lie to us. He seems remarkably thorough. I trust him at his word."

Harriett stared into the fire. "Isn't it possible Blake parked his carriage blocks away on purpose? I don't know how open a secret his warehouse is, but if he keeps his smuggled silks and lace in there, he would not want people to associate it with him. Or so I would think."

Having thought hard about this through half the night, Katherine had almost certainly struck upon her next suspect. In fact, the longer she contemplated it, the more certain she was that was the case. However, she was reluctant to release another theory into the air. What if she was wrong yet again? But if she wasted more time, Wayland and Lord Annandale might solve the case ahead of them.

Sitting here and worrying about it wouldn't solve the murder, either. Katherine set Emma on the ground and stood. The other two women in the room glanced up, giving her their undivided attention. Harriet cut off in mid-sentence.

"There's one other person we haven't considered. Someone who might be involved and who I believe has lied to us," Katherine said.

"Who?"

"Madame Manteau. You saw the peculiar way she acted when pretending she didn't know Mr. Blake. Now that we know he is a smuggler, I'm certain that hers is one of the shops he uses to make his income legitimate. It is the only reason she could sell such expensive fabrics at so economical a price. And since she's already lied to us..."

Pru's face brightened. "Of course! If Ellie knew of the smuggling, then she might know of Manteau's involvement."

"And she did have a nightdress from the shop, so it's likely she was there," Harriett said.

Katherine smiled. "What do you say we take a stroll and call upon Madame Manteau once again? I don't know about you, but I would like some answers."

THE DOOR RATTLED on its hinges from the bitter wind as the three women stepped into Madame Manteau's shop. The sole customer inside hurried to dole out the necessary coins, gather her paper-wrapped purchase in her arms, and elbow her way through the three women to the exit. Curious. It was almost as if the customers, too, knew that the wares could not have been legally obtained.

The moment the door closed behind the customer, Katherine crossed to Madame Manteau. However, with only a suspicion and no proof, Katherine hesitated to accuse her. If she spoke out of turn and frightened the woman out of London, Ellie's murderer might remain at large. She had to be clever about her questions.

As Harriet toured around the shop, inspecting the goods offered and pausing over the bolts of silk and lace with a raised eyebrow, Pru stopped in front of the shears. She chose a pair and opened them to examine the edge. According to Lyle, the murder weapon was short but wickedly sharp. A smaller pair of these shears fit that description almost perfectly. Katherine's heart stilled. She knew Madame Manteau knew more than she was saying, but could she be the killer?

Pulling her attention away from the shears, Katherine pinned Madame Manteau with a knowing stare. She had won this battle. The woman seemed to recognize her victory as well, from the paleness of her cheeks and the way she flitted her gaze from woman to woman without speaking a word.

If she didn't opt to greet her customers, that left Katherine to control the conversation. "Hello again, madame. I'm afraid I have a bone of contention to pick with you."

The woman drew herself up to her meager height, indignation on her face. "What ill could you find with my wares?"

"Not with your wares, madame. With the lies you told when I was last in here."

She scoffed, meeting Katherine's gaze boldly. "I do not know what you are speaking of."

She could feign a language barrier all she liked. Katherine knew better. She smiled, but it was a far from friendly expression. "Then allow me to refresh your memory. We were speaking of a young woman you sold a nightgown to, a petite blond woman by the name of Ellie Simpson. *Je parle français*. I can repeat in French, if you're having difficulty."

The shopkeeper brushed her finger across her upper lip, a telling sign. "*Non*. I can understand you fine."

Of course she could, considering that she was native to England rather than France.

Katherine carried on. "When I was last here, you informed me that you didn't know my friend, Ellie."

The woman turned red in the face, drawing herself up. "I don't. What reason would I have to lie?"

Katherine raised her eyebrows. "Why? Because she's dead. And she was killed in an alley mere steps away from here. So, tell me again. Where were you the night of the fire?"

"What fire?" Madame Manteau said, fake French accent slipping.

"The fire at the Hound and Ale Pub. Every shopkeeper hereabouts recalls it. You were all in danger of the flames spreading."

Dropping her gaze, the shopkeeper turned away to fiddle with the coins from her last customer. "My grandson spends the day several streets north and..." She scowled. "What business is it of yours?"

Katherine meandered to the stack of lace next to the silk. "This is very fine lace. Unusual, considering the taxes."

"I have very fine sources. I assure you, it is all authentic."

Katherine let the fabric drop and moved closer to the woman once more. She might have been a murderer, but with her friends at her back, Katherine felt safe. Besides, Pru was guarding the shears.

"If that were true, you could not afford to be selling them for the amount you are. I know you lied about where you were the night of the fire. The night Ellie Simpson was killed — with a weapon very similar to those scissors."

Madame Manteau recoiled. "*Zut alors!* Surely you don't think I killed her?"

Katherine raised her eyebrows but let her expression answer for her.

The mature woman wrung her hands. She

dropped her accent and whispered, "I would never kill anyone."

Pru's eyes widened. Had she believed that false accent?

Katherine pressed on. "No? If you didn't kill anyone, then why did you lie to me?"

The woman cast a wary glance to the door. When no other customers intruded on the moment, she admitted, "I know Ellie. That wretched girl was blackmailing me because she discovered I sell fabrics for Mr. Blake. He is my source. I've never asked, but at these prices, I doubt he's acquired them by legitimate means."

Ha! So Katherine had been right. Ellie was blackmailing Manteau. Did that mean she was not blackmailing Mr. Blake? Or was she blackmailing both of them? Triumph surged within Katherine, so hot and strong that she nearly grinned. If she did, she would lose her advantage against her suspect, who was shaken now.

So shaken that she continued to babble, her accent a far-off memory as she beseeched Katherine and her friends in turn. "You don't know how difficult it is for a woman to make a living these days. But I promise you, I did not kill Ellie. When she came to call that day, I paid her and sent her on her way as usual. It was more profitable for me to do that than to try to thwart her, anyway."

Katherine exchanged a glance with Pru, wondering if she should believe the woman. She couldn't tell from Pru's expression whether she believed her or not.

Madame Manteau added, "Sometimes in lieu of cash, Ellie would choose an article of clothing that I had prepared. That's how she came by the nightdress."

"You said she came asking for payment that day?"

Bald horror crossed the woman's face, aging her by ten years. Apparently, she'd assumed that Katherine had already determined Ellie's whereabouts on the day she had died. "She did. But she took coin only, no clothing."

It was a pretty story but one that Katherine couldn't verify. Who but Madame Manteau would know of the blackmail? And why was Ellie's reticule empty when she was found? Katherine doubted that the police had taken it, and the odds of her death having been a robbery with all this going on seemed unlikely.

Perhaps someone else would be able to place Ellie, alive, leaving the shop. "Was anyone else here in the store with you? Can you prove that she left here alive?"

"I work here alone, but—" As Katherine turned away, she flung up her hands. "Wait! From here, she went across the street to Mr. Wright's shop. He's a cobbler. You can go over right now and ask him. I'm certain he'll recall her."

Katherine paused, but half turned to raise an eyebrow in the woman's direction. "And how do we know you didn't follow her after she visited the cobbler?"

Madame Manteau's face twisted with desperation. "I was here the entire time. You can ask Mr. Wright. It was just starting to rain when she left, and the thunderstorm took another half hour or more before it fell upon us. I was here finishing the dress I was working on, and it was Mr. Wright who rushed over to tell me about the fire. We left the shop together, and I don't know what became of Ellie after she left his. I suppose you'll have to ask him."

Did she dare believe the woman? Katherine might not have a choice. She'd already dug too deep with her questions to allow Madame Manteau to rest easy. She knew about the smuggling, the blackmail... At her guess, unless Katherine was able to convince Lyle to send a colleague to watch the shop, the seamstress would take the next ship out of London. Perhaps she'd even see the France she was so fond of mentioning in order to hook customers.

"Then why did you lie to us earlier?" Katherine asked.

Madame Manteau's brows drew together. "Of course I would lie. I knew that Ellie was killed, and if anyone found out she was blackmailing me that I would be a suspect. But I swear, I am not her killer."

If she was the murderer, she might slip away, and Katherine could do nothing to stop her. So she bluffed. In a low, threatening tone, she said, "If I were you, *madame*, I would continue to run your shop as usual. If you run, we will find you."

Then she turned on her heel to verify the woman's tale.

CHAPTER TWENTY

M r. Wright's cobbler's shop was a small, dingy affair compared to that of Madame Manteau. In the front room, there was a small stand displaying a variety of shoes he had made, likely to the specifications of customers who had not been able to pay when the final product had been ready. The sizes ranged from children's to a large man's boot, and the styles were as eclectic. But the single display was the only indication of his livelihood. A closed door likely led to a workshop or a storeroom where he kept his supplies. The walls were drab and a rusty brown that made the interior look dark despite the tallow candle in the corner. A bench rested along that wall, where the cobbler now worked by shaping the sole of a yet-unfinished shoe.

From the size, it looked to belong to a woman. The old man, with his craggy face, squinted in the light of the candle and shaved another layer off the pointed heel.

When he paused to examine his work, Katherine smoothed the distaste from her expression, born of the fatty stench of the candle, and stepped forward. "Excuse me, sir. I'm hoping you might be able to help us."

The man looked up, his eyes widening as he took in her apparel. Despite Madame Manteau's shop across the street, he must have been able to discern Katherine's wealth, perhaps due to Harriet's presence. Or maybe the man knew her from her resemblance to her father.

"Of course, my lady. It would be my pleasure to be of service." With bones so old they creaked, he levered himself to his feet and made a bow. "If you're here looking for shoes, I am overjoyed to be of service."

Inwardly, Katherine cringed. He seemed like such a genuine old man that she fought the urge to buy a pair of shoes from him even though she had a cobbler she was more than content with. However, she was here solving a murder. Her soft heart would get her nowhere.

"A friend of mine bought shoes from you a few

months ago. I'm hoping you might remember them, or her?"

The man rubbed his hands together. "I'll do my best, but my memory isn't what it once was…"

A diplomatic way of saying that he didn't typically recall his clientele. Nevertheless, Katherine described Ellie — or, at the very least, she described Ellie's sister. Thinking back to the tattered rags Sarah had kept in the box, she added, "She would have been wearing a blue dress that day. I believe it was an auspicious day when she came in, the same day the Hound and Ale Pub burned?"

Mr. Wright's eyes widened. He passed his hand over the whiskers on his chin. "I remember that night. The girl…" He frowned, stopping to organize his tools by length as he thought. It might have been an evasive gesture, done to buy him the time to lie.

Katherine steeled herself.

When he turned back, he nodded decisively. "Yes, I do think I remember such a girl. She was here to buy herself a pair of silk shoes…or were they satin?" He shook his head. "I don't sell many of them, and she nearly bought another pair for her sister, but the ones she bought for herself took every coin in her purse." He sighed, glancing toward the door. "The sky turned dark frighteningly fast. She tried to leave before the storm hit and promised to come back, but... she never did." The lines in his face deepened. "She left just in time as the rain started shortly after. I was worried she might have caught a chill on her way home."

Unfortunately, Ellie had caught a far more woeful end than a cold.

Katherine asked, "Did she meet someone when she left the shop?"

"Not that I recall."

Pru chimed in. "Did you see someone following her?"

He shook his head, gray sprigs of his hair bouncing as he did. "I'm afraid not. When I looked out after her, all I saw were a few ladies running for cover in their carriages or stopping in shop doorways as the rain worsened. That was quite the storm. Even these old bones rattled from that thunder."

Emboldened by the response, Pru stepped closer. "And what happened after that? Did you close up your shop and go home?"

The old man lifted a bony finger. "I was about to leave. Not likely many people will come into the shop with the thunder drowning out the sound of your own voice. But a boy came running up the street screaming that the pub was on fire! I saw the light on in Madame Manteau's shop, and I hurried to collect her, in case she didn't know. We were both afraid that the fire might spread up to our shops, so we ran down to watch the fire brigade put it out. It was chaos."

Katherine opened her mouth but shut it again. His tale corroborated that of the seamstress's — and it placed Ellie alive leaving the shop. Unless the shoe store merchant and Madame Manteau had killed Ellie together, Katherine was once again left without a suspect.

And with little time to find one.

CHAPTER TWENTY-ONE

If Katherine didn't find a new suspect and quickly, Wayland would solve this murder ahead of her. She knew he was a good investigator. After all, he had helped her in the past. But she had to prove that she was better, and she didn't have a lot of time left.

Turning on her side in bed, Katherine swiped at her gritty eyes. She'd spent half the night jotting down every clue she knew and trying desperately to add them all up. The problem was, nothing seemed to align. Someone somewhere must be lying to them, and she hadn't been keen enough to discover who. She was missing something, some vital clue that tied everything together.

Unless Ellie's murder had been a coincidence, after all...

No. She had been blackmailing Mr. Blake and Madame Manteau. Katherine knew it. Besides, the man in the shoe store said she'd spent her last coin on the shoes, so robbery couldn't be a motive. It *had* to be more than coincidence.

With a whine, Emma trundled forward on the mattress and licked Katherine's cheek. Absently, Katherine patted her on the head.

The door creaked open and shut again. "You're awake."

Katherine sighed at the sound of Harriet's voice. "I can't sleep. What time is it?"

The gap in the curtains widened, spilling light into the room. "Scarcely eight of the morning."

Katherine had fallen into bed less than four hours ago. Her eyes ached, and she cracked a yawn.

"Have you thought of anything else?" Harriet had spent the better part of the night awake with Katherine as they considered every clue they had learned. When neither of them had been able to puzzle out an answer, Katherine had nearly gone to Papa for help. But he and Susanna had already gone to bed, and she hadn't wanted to disturb them.

"No. I'm not sure I slept a wink for thinking about it."

"If you aren't going to sleep, why don't you dress

and come down for bit of breakfast? After you've filled your belly, you might think better."

Katherine heaved a sigh but swung her legs out of bed. The warm floorboards beneath indicated that the kitchen had long since bustled into activity. She shivered in the cooler air but stood and silently followed Harriet's direction.

"Is that what you tried?"

Harriet scoffed. "The food hasn't hit my belly yet to give me that stroke of inspiration we need. Now stay still so I can tie your laces. And make no mistake, princess—" She brandished a finger at the dog. "You're next."

Emma dove off the bed to hide beneath it. Smirking, Katherine held her tongue. Harriet was in a poor mood this morning, it seemed.

Ten minutes later, Harriet was stoically brushing out Katherine's hair when the door opened again.

Pru, her hair haphazardly piled up off of her neck and her eyes just as bloodshot as Katherine's, poked her head into the room. "Oh good, you're awake. The butler let me in. I couldn't sleep."

Harriet sighed and set down the hairbrush. "Why don't I put on some tea?"

HALF AN HOUR LATER, they were still arguing over the clues, far more energized for having had the tea.

Katherine shook her head. "Mr. Blake has an alibi."

Pru jabbed her finger through the air. "He also has the best motive. He is rich enough to hire someone to kill Ellie, isn't he?"

"By that logic, Madame Manteau has every bit as much of a motive. She admitted to Ellie blackmailing her."

Pru breathed out a gusty sigh. "But Madame Manteau has an alibi, as well. A better one."

Harriet fiddled with the cups on their saucers, refilling each one and adding sugar lumps. "Someone must be lying."

In that, Katherine couldn't agree more.

Pru pointed out, "Lord Quinbury cannot be trusted. Who's to say he was at this card game with Mr. Blake? Perhaps he is only trying to save his new business venture by lying for Blake and claiming to have been there."

Gritting her teeth, Katherine shook her head. "I told you, I trust Mr. Pell. Besides, it wasn't Quinbury that he interviewed in order to corroborate his story. He tracked down Quinbury's former valet, the man he turned out after he lost a great sum at that very card game. He isn't, I take it, very good at playing loo. I can send Mr. Pell a note asking him the name and direction of the man he interviewed so we can speak with him directly, but I doubt this is a case of Mr. Blake having asked Lord Quinbury to lie for him. Tarnation, Quinbury is a duke!"

Harriet suggested, "Not Mr. Blake, then. Perhaps Madame Manteau had Mr. Wright lie for her!"

Katherine considered the information. "Why would he do that?"

Pru nodded. "Everything Madame Manteau claimed turned out to be correct. After leaving her shop, Ellie went into Mr. Wright's to buy a pair of shoes. And then Mr. Wright collected Madame Manteau, and they went to see the fire. Neither of them could have killed Ellie, right?"

Katherine nodded.

Scrunching her face, Harriet asked, "If that's the case, where are the shoes? Did you find them in her sister's possession? Bow Street would have given them with the rest of her things, wouldn't they?"

Katherine frowned as she thought of the box Sarah had carried downstairs to show them. After a moment, she shook her head. A pair of silk shoes would have been noticeable. The only thing in the box provided her by Bow Street had been a pair of serviceable shoes, ones Ellie might have worn to work.

"You're right. Ellie didn't have the shoes on her when she was found."

"Perhaps it is a robbery, then," Pru suggested.

A woman dead simply so that someone could steal her new shoes? What a travesty.

Katherine nodded. "You could be right. But Madame Manteau has a strong motive, and those shears could have been the murder weapon. Money can be a great motivator. And did you see Mr. Wright's shop? Perhaps she paid him to lie for her. He looks as though he could use the money."

Harriet raised her eyebrows. "Or perhaps she blackmailed him into doing it. There's a lot of that going around recently."

Katherine didn't want to jump to that conclusion, though it was possible. Still, something about this new theory didn't sit right with her. Mr. Wright had provided such a detailed account of Ellie's visit that she didn't think it had been concocted. Usually, she was good at telling fact from fiction. Perhaps her impression of him was getting in the way of her good judgment. Simply because he looked like a kindly grandfather didn't mean he didn't hold a sinister heart.

Movement at the corner of her eye caught her

attention. Eager for the distraction, Katherine met her stepmother with a warm smile.

It was matched by the devious look on Susanna's face. She sailed into the room, brandishing a letter. Stopping at Katherine's side, she dangled the parchment in front of Katherine's nose. "A letter for you."

Katherine snatched it out of the air. "Who is it from?" The paper was thick, the ruby wax seal stiff.

"It's from Lord Conyers' solicitor. It must be regarding the townhouse!"

Katherine's heart skipped a beat. She stood, searching the room. "Where's your erasing knife?"

Her stepmother was already halfway across the room. As she reached the small writing desk in the corner, she pulled open the top drawer. When Katherine reached her, she handed the erasing knife to her with a flourish. Katherine used the sharp edge to pry up the seal. She applied more force as the wax proved stiff and reluctant. When it popped off, the short, sharp blade nicked the edge of her thumb.

"Ouch!" She stuck the digit in her mouth and sucked hard, hoping to stem the coppery blood. Those erasing knives proved wickedly sharp! The handle slipped from her fingers, clattering to the floor, where Emma tried to sniff it. Katherine held her at bay with a foot, lest she hurt herself.

"Oh, dear! Give that here, let me see."

Katherine offered her thumb as Susanna fished a handkerchief from her bodice.

Her stepmother *tsk*ed as she examined the wound. "I don't think it's too deep, but you'd better hold this here until it stops bleeding." She applied pressure to the wound, making Katherine wince and drop her gaze to the floor.

Where the erasing knife had landed, the inch-long blade was wet with her blood. As she prodded it with her toe, she gasped.

"Quick, Pru. Send a note to Lord Annandale. We need to meet immediately. I know who the killer is!"

CHAPTER TWENTY-TWO

Anticipation made every muscle in Katherine's body sing as she stood in Lord Annandale's sitting room, eyeing the other six people now seated and staring at her. Pru and Annandale had claimed most of the settee, sitting near to each other and cooing in one another's ears. Even outside of her parents' home, the cooing appeared to be an epidemic. Katherine couldn't imagine acting that way with anyone. So emotional, especially in public? She shook her head.

McTavish blurted, "Och, lass. Are ye planning to wait until we die of old age before ye tell us why you called us here?"

She smiled despite the impertinence. She let her gaze trail over the company to rest squarely on

Wayland. Looking him in the eye, she announced triumphantly, "I've solved the case."

Pru broke apart from Annandale on the settee to arch her eyebrow. Despite having settled the final clues in her mind when they had been together, Katherine had kept her secrets until now, wanting to reveal her victory to everyone at once.

Katherine ignored her, informing the room, "I will now tell you who did it and why. I called Lyle here so that he can then go and arrest the killer."

Lyle leaned back in his chair, his expression astounded. "I'd say that's decidedly mature for you. Don't you usually prefer to coerce the confession yourself?"

Katherine thought back to the last two times she had confronted murderers. Both times, she had nearly been killed. "I think it might be better for the professionals to handle the arrest this time."

Wayland grunted, but Katherine couldn't decide whether he agreed or not.

Pru pouted. "I wanted to confront the killer." She glared at Lyle. "Why should Lyle have all the fun?"

Katherine stifled a sigh. Evenly, she answered, "I would like nothing more. However, it won't do to let on we are detectives, will it? I'm not giving the credit of my solving the case to Wayland and Lord Annandale."

Wayland smirked, but he didn't argue the point. And neither did Pru.

Pru's eyes gleamed with mischief. "Well, I suppose I have one consolation."

"And what is that, lass?" Annandale brushed his fingers over her upper arms as he asked.

She tilted her face to meet his, her smile widening. "I won't have to clobber the killer over the head this time to save Katherine!"

Katherine bristled. It was true, that Pru had clobbered the killer the last two times, but Katherine hardly *needed* her to do that. She would have gotten out of the situation on her own in time. However, her answer to Pru was true as well. They still needed to preserve her reputation, or she would be thrust from the very society she used to search for clues.

"Are you ready to hear what I have to say?"

"Yes," both Harriet and McTavish said at once.

Katherine took their encouragement at its surface value and turned to Wayland. "Your assumption of blackmail was only partially correct."

He barked a laugh. "*My* assumption? I'm fairly certain it was your assumption."

Had she suggested it first, or had he? She couldn't recall. Mouth twisting, she inclined her head to him for the point. "Perhaps. Blackmail, you see, was at the heart of this murder, but not for the reasons we thought. Ellie Simpson was blackmailing not only Mr. Blake, but also Madame Manteau."

McTavish stretched his legs out in front of him and crossed them at the ankle. The movement brought him inches closer to Harriet, seated next to him. "So, which one did her in?"

Harriet made a short, impatient sound. "Let her explain, you brute!"

He gave her his most charming, womanizing smile.

Katherine continued. "At first, I thought Mr. Blake must be the culprit."

Wayland made a short, unimpressed sound. "The obvious suspect," he said under his breath.

She ignored him. Instead, she let her eyes drift over the others, especially Lyle, who would be acting on her information. "We thought he was taking Ellie to bed, along with numerous others. We toyed with the idea of the culprit being another maid, jealous of the attention and gifts he bestowed upon her."

McTavish narrowed his eyes at Harriet, suspicious. "Och now, how did ye come tae learn that?"

Ignoring him, Harriet arranged her skirts around the dog, who seemed content to lay her head on her paws and turn to watch the volley of speakers as they argued. She gave him a sly look out of the corner of her eye. "I have my ways, same as you."

"Do ye now?"

Lyle, disgruntled, spoke overtop of them. "If she was blackmailing Mr. Blake, the gifts were likely to have come from that, not from any lingering affection on his part."

Katherine nodded to him, hoping her agreement would ease the black look on his face. "Precisely so. We ruled out the maid before we discovered that Mr. Blake was involved with smuggling." She inclined her head to Wayland, who had uncovered that bit of information. "However, *he* could not have been the killer since he was with Lord Quinbury that afternoon and into the night. I haven't checked Mr. Pell's investigative work, but it can easily be done. He'll have the name of the valet he interviewed, and I'm certain there were more people playing loo that day than only Mr. Blake and Lord Quinbury." She nodded to Lyle. "I can help you in checking that, if you see fit."

He nodded back to her but didn't interrupt her. "Pell works for Silver's Detective Agency, doesn't he?"

"I believe so."

"I've worked with their agents from time to time when we cross paths. They're capable sorts. I'm sure his information is correct."

Lord Annandale bristled, nearly levitating off the settee before Pru laid a restraining hand on his arm. "No fair, lass! That lead about Lord Quinbury was ours. *We* tasked Mr. Pell to look into it for us."

Sweetly, Katherine smiled at him. "Then perhaps you should have done your own investigating, rather than hiring a third party to do it for you. Is that fair?"

Lord Annandale looked at Wayland, as if expecting him to protest. After all, the wager was between Wayland and Katherine, not the respective teams. They hadn't made a rule about not involving outside sources, particularly when the work to be done involved sitting outside a warehouse for hours to confirm that it did, in fact, belong to Mr. Blake. However, she could argue that it violated their code of honor.

In case he, too, reprimanded her for the use of the clue—which she still considered to be fair game—Katherine carried on. "And Lord Annandale, pray tell, where was it that you discovered the information that led you to set Mr. Pell on Mr. Blake's warehouse?"

Annandale puffed up, proud. "We were at White's."

"And you think it's fair that you can get information from a men's club that we women have no access to?" She stared him down, forcing him to concede the point. When he looked away to Wayland again, though the latter held his tongue, she continued, "In any case, we discovered that information simultaneously at the Royal Society meeting. I didn't steal it out from under you."

His voice as serene as a pond on a summer's day, Wayland said, "She has a point."

Lord Annandale grumbled darkly, but he settled back on the settee next to his fiancée. He didn't protest further, and Katherine paused long enough to make certain of that. She had a story to tell, after all.

Katherine carried on. She turned her attention back to Wayland for a moment, wondering if his logic had followed the same route as hers. "Once I learned about the smuggling, it didn't take long to uncover that Madame Manteau was involved in that, as well."

"Madame Manteau, you say?" Lyle pulled a notebook from his pocket and turned to a fresh page, making a note.

Helpfully, Katherine added, "She's a seamstress. Her shop is down the street from the Hound and Ale Pub. I think you'll find her cooperative if you need her to testify against Mr. Blake, provided you're lenient on her error. I found her shop while I was on my way to look at the crime scene. After Ellie's sister"—she glanced at Wayland, emphasizing the fact that her approach had proved of some use despite his initial derision—"showed us the expensive nightgown that Ellie had had in her possession. It was from Madame Manteau's shop. As it turns out, she makes a distinctive mark in all of her garments, which made her easier to find."

"Do you think you'd be able to replicate the mark for me?" Lyle asked as he tucked his book away.

Katherine nodded. "It's fairly simple. She has it on the sign above her shop door, as well." She turned to the others. She had their attention, though the men wore identical expressions of polite boredom. Even McTavish appeared more interested in polishing a scuff on his boot on the carpet than looking at her.

Apparently none of them enjoyed losing.

Katherine, however, adored the victory. She smiled. "The first time I visited the shop, we noticed that Madame Manteau has sharp, narrow shears in the front to cut the cloth. The same type that might have killed Ellie."

Wayland made a strangled sound. When she glanced at him, he passed a hand over his mouth but not soon enough to hide the smirk on his face.

She raised her eyebrows at him. "Do you have something to add?"

His face solemn again, he waved her along. "No, carry on. I had a frog in my throat."

Katherine glared at him before she turned to the rest of the room. "However, the killer was not Madame Manteau."

McTavish threw up his hands, betraying that he had, in fact, been listening. "Well, lass, who was it then? Get on with it!"

Pru explained, "Madame Manteau had an alibi. We verified it." With a gleam in her eye, she looked sideways at her fiancé. "Did you have her on your suspect list?"

Looking lost, Lord Annandale turned to Wayland. At Wayland's shrug, he mumbled, "We considered her..."

For some reason, Katherine doubted that. If not for the stitching on the inside of Ellie's nightgown, she would not have known that Madame Manteau existed. It was conceivable they had followed the smuggling angle to discover which shops were associated with Mr. Blake, but that would have taken a lot of time. Perhaps that was why Wayland had employed Mr. Pell.

Pru huffed. "Right. Well, we deduced that it wasn't her. Go on, Katherine, tell him the rest."

Smiling at her friend, Katherine resumed her tale.

"Madame Manteau could not have killed Ellie. Although Ellie did visit her shop that day, she was in good health when she left and ventured across the street to the cobbler shop. I checked with Mr. Wright, and he verifies that she came in and left alive. It wasn't but a few moments after she left that they got word of the fire. He went across the street to collect Madame Manteau, and they both watched fearfully, lest the flames spread to their shops."

Katherine looked down at her hands, reliving that disheartening information. "After we verified Madame Manteau's alibi, I have to admit to being stumped. She and Mr. Blake were the only two who would have known about and wanted the blackmail stopped, or so I thought. But then I realized that one other person had a very important stake in the blackmail."

McTavish sat straighter. "Who?"

She smiled but didn't answer him directly. Letting her gaze drift over the gathering once more, she continued her tale. "After I realized one more person suffered from the blackmail, it wasn't hard to put two and two together. You see, when we were talking to the servants at Mr. Blake's house, we discovered that Mr. Blake's shoes were burned."

The men didn't look impressed. Katherine carried on regardless. It was a vital clue.

"It makes sense, because he was indeed at the fire. However, Mrs. Blake also had a pair of shoes that needed attending. They had been there for several months, and they were quite remarkable. Those shoes were silk, and water stained."

Lord Annandale turned to his betrothed with a raised eyebrow. "That seems what ye'd expect, were ye walking around on wet ground. How is it relevant?"

Katherine grinned. "Ah, but it is! You see, the shoes were only water stained on the *tops*. If she was wearing them, the water stains would have been on the bottom." Katherine lifted her foot to show them her own shoes, which she'd been wearing when she stepped in the puddle. The water stain left an obvious line on the sides of the shoes. The tops were fine.

Impatient, McTavish grunted. "So?"

Harriet made a face at him. "Ellie bought a pair of shoes from the cobbler. But the shoes were not found with the body."

McTavish, Wayland, and Annandale exchanged a look of surprise. Katherine grinned, satisfied that she had come to a conclusion they hadn't considered.

That was when utter chaos broke out. The Scots spoke on top of one another, each trying to convince her that her lead was false. The voices rose in a crescendo that ended with McTavish on his feet, trying to tower over Katherine and failing.

He scoffed. "Ye've made your base claim because Mrs. Blake has soiled shoes? Yer mad!"

Lord Annandale nodded, though he didn't stand. "Even Lyle, loyal to you though he is, couldn't act on a fancy like that."

Katherine held up her hands, stopping the two men in midsentence. The cascade of their voices rang in her ears as they heeded her. She glared from one to the other in turn. Biting off her words, she said, "In itself, perhaps that would not be conclusive. But there are other clues, and they all add up."

McTavish looked at her askance. "Go on."

"Amongst Ellie's things was also a reticule which was stained on one side. Ellie's sister said that was because Ellie fell on the reticule when she was killed. She was killed before it started raining, and the reticule only got wet when the police started to examine the crime scene. The same likely happened with the shoes. That's why they were wet only on the tops."

"And did you verify with the cobbler that those were in fact the shoes Ellie purchased?" Lyle asked.

"No, since I couldn't very well confiscate the shoes, I will leave that to the police. However, there is also another clue that I think will be even more telling." Katherine paused dramatically.

"Do tell," Wayland said dryly.

Katherine continued, "You see, Ellie used to open the mail for Mrs. Blake."

McTavish sighed, apparently disgusted at how long it was taking Katherine to reveal the clues. He dropped into his chair heavily, making it creak. Katherine ignored his impatience.

"When Ellie died, that duty fell to Rita, one of the other maids. In fact, the same maid we thought might be capable of killing Ellie. But that wasn't the case," she assured Lyle. "You see, Rita has a deformity in her hand. No strength or dexterity to it, and she is unable to open the letters, too. So she had Harriet's friend, Gabrielle, do it. However, according to Gabrielle, the erasing knife used to break the seals has been missing since Ellie died."

Understanding dawned on McTavish's face, mingled with disgust. "The murder weapon!"

Katherine held up her thumb, evidence that these knives were wickedly sharp. "Indeed. I cut myself with one today."

Lord Annandale still didn't appear convinced. "Why would Mrs. Blake steal Ellie's shoes? She could have bought her own."

Katherine raised her eyebrows. "Could she? Mr. Blake is a notorious skinflint. Mrs. Blake likes the finer things in life. Money is also the reason she killed Ellie. You see, although Mr. Blake might not have shared news of the blackmail with his wife, Mrs. Blake was having an affair with their driver. The driver must have guessed about the blackmail, having stopped for Ellie up in the carriage one day while Mr. Blake paid the sum. Once Mrs. Blake learned of the blackmail, Ellie's demise was certain. She would not have wanted it to continue, as it would mean even less money for her.

"One of the shopkeepers near the Hound and Ale Pub saw the Blake carriage near the scene of the crime, on Young Street, during the storm. However, it was not Mr. Blake who took it. I'm sure, upon digging deeper, we will find that he went to his warehouse in Lord Quinbury's carriage. The Blake carriage in that area was due to Mrs. Blake, hence why the driver denied being there—he was protecting his lover. Mrs. Blake followed Ellie intending to kill her. It's possible she knew that Ellie collected the blackmail money from Madame Manteau on a certain day every week. She followed to put a stop to the blackmail ... and took a little souvenir for herself."

By the end of her tale, even Lord Annandale

looked impressed. He gathered Pru's hand in his and gave her an adoring look. "I must say, you ladies are fine detectives." He narrowed his eyes at Wayland, who didn't look at him. "Och, Wayland. Did you have no idea of this? I thought you mentioned—"

"I hadn't the foggiest," Wayland said, sharply and quickly. He got to his feet and bowed to Katherine, Pru, and Harriet in turn. "It looks like you ladies have outdone us. You have won our wager."

Harriet squealed in glee. Disturbed, Emma jumped from her lap and bounded to a quieter corner of the room. It left Harriet unprepared for McTavish's surprisingly gracious admission of defeat. He kissed the back of her hand, forfeiting the game to her. Harriet froze a moment, only pulling her hand free when Lyle loudly cleared his throat and pronounced himself as having had confidence in their team the entire time.

Pru grinned from ear to ear as she turned to Lord Annandale. Whether to share her joy or console him in his defeat, Katherine didn't know.

She, on the other hand, raised her eyebrow at Wayland.

Hadn't he capitulated a little bit too easily? While the Scotsmen had been trying to discount her clues, he had been curiously silent. And why had he cut

Lord Annandale off before he'd spoken his full sentence?

Katherine suspected that Wayland wasn't surprised with her deductions — because he'd had the same ones. If that was true, why cede the victory to her? He could have argued for a draw.

Could he have *let* her win? No. It would be utterly unlike him. Wayland was...

Some days, she didn't know what kind of man Wayland was, despite what her father said.

Leaning closer, he said conspiratorially, "I thought you would be happier to have bested me."

Startled from her thoughts, Katherine smiled at him. She had won this match, hadn't she? She thanked him with a gracious nod, but mischief stole over her heart. "Oh, I'm ecstatic. I am *so* looking forward to Lady Cabot's ball tomorrow night, aren't you? It will be lovely to see you dressed up as Joe the Jester."

He gave a mock groan and placed his hand over his heart as if wounded.

CHAPTER TWENTY-THREE

K atherine's veins hummed with the thrill of success. Unable to keep from smiling, she reached forward to squeeze Lyle's arm. "That's wonderful news. Thank you for telling me."

With a shrug, he plunged his hands into the pockets of his greatcoat. "I thought you'd want to know what happened." The light of the streetlamp passed over his face as he craned it to look down Mayfair Street toward the ring of carriages disgorging their occupants in front of a looming townhouse. "I trust you'll pass along the information to Wayland?"

"Are you certain you don't want to come in? I'm sure I can gain you entrance."

"Attend a Twelfth Night ball?" He shuddered. "Not on your life. Besides, I had a breakthrough on one of my inventions. I want to get back to it while I have some free time."

Katherine nodded. "Very well. I'll let everyone know what's happened."

The information fogged her head as they parted ways. Snow fell in fat flakes around her, but she barely felt the whispers of cold as they settled on her skin. She wove in between the other costumed guests and up the stairs, her persona — the Roman goddess Minerva — firmly in place. The butler paused only to take her cloak as she returned, recognizing her at once and ushering her down the corridor and into Lady Cabot's ballroom.

The ballroom was a spectacle of candlelight and frosted decorations. Tricks of the light made it almost seem as though the snow persisted indoors, where it was hot enough to make her break out in a sweat. Chatter rose and fell in the crush as people elbowed their way past acquaintances and greeted friends. In the center, couples bowed and straightened like the wind bending blades of grass.

Not for the first time, Katherine found herself grateful for Wayland's pronounced height. She might not have found him otherwise, although, in his blue-and-red-striped doublet and hat, perhaps he couldn't be missed.

Next to him, Lord Annandale looked almost staid in his chosen persona. He and Pru had elected to come as Anthony and Cleopatra. Like Katherine, they'd left the traditional harlequins to other attendees in favor of something more original.

When Katherine reached them, Pru was trying to entice Wayland to ask someone to dance. Katherine didn't hear who, but she pitied the poor woman. She had danced with Wayland before, and although he was a passable dancer, his outfit would undoubtedly cause a stir and embarrass the poor woman, even if he filled out the puffed shoulders nicely.

When she reached the group, Pru widened her eyes and switched tactics. "Katherine! I hadn't realized you'd arrived. You look divine. Doesn't she, Wayland?"

"She always does."

Pru snorted and covered her mouth delicately with a hand. Katherine glared at them both, certain they were poking fun at her usual wardrobe. It seemed to be a favorite topic of Pru's.

"I was outside, speaking with Lyle. Bow Street made an arrest today, and he wanted to inform me of the results."

Pru's smirk fell from her face at once. "Oh? What did he say?"

"It took some doing, but with Mr. Blake under

suspicion for smuggling, the magistrate was willing to overlook his wealth and have the house searched. They found the murder weapon — the erasing knife — in Mrs. Blake's writing desk in her bedchamber. It was thrust into the furthest corner, and it looks to have been cleaned, but she couldn't get properly into the crevasse of the carved handle. They found blood, or something that looks very much like it. It was enough to convince her to confess."

Lord Annandale shook his head. "A tragedy, it is."

Wayland raised his eyebrows. "You are correct about the murderer, but were you correct about the motive?"

Katherine laughed. "You've already conceded the wager to me. What would you do if you found that the motive was wrong? Take off your costume?"

Color climbed up his neck. "I think not."

Katherine grinned at him. She'd never made him blush before. Teasing him was surprisingly fun.

At least until he cocked one eyebrow and added, "There are far too many buttons on the outfit. I would need help."

This time, it was she who blushed. She'd never seen him unclothed, of course, but while in Bath he had bathed in the public King's Bath. A wet shirt left little to the imagination.

Katherine cleared her throat. "The motive was correct as well. Mrs. Blake killed Ellie because Ellie was siphoning away their money. The constant threat of her tattling to the authorities about Mr. Blake's smuggling was too much to bear, since Mrs. Blake did not want to lose the entire fortune."

Raising an eyebrow, Wayland shook his head. "And yet, now that Bow Street knows of the smuggling, they are undoubtedly working to reveal it. I have no doubt they will prevail against Mr. Blake, and Madame Manteau, as well."

"Lyle is on the case, and I have every faith in his abilities."

Wayland looked thoughtful, but he murmured, "Lyle is a capable fellow. I'm sure he will have no trouble bringing them to justice."

The tone of respect in Wayland's voice surprised her. He and Lyle had worked together before, but Katherine didn't realize Wayland had such generous feelings toward the Bow Street Runner. She'd always thought Wayland was the type to think himself superior, but then, he had given credit to Lyle before, even though the credit had been mostly Wayland's.

Wayland slipped his arm around her waist, pulling her away from the dance floor and closer to the heat of his body. "Watch yourself."

A couple waltzed past, so close their passing stirred Katherine's skirts. When she looked over her shoulder, she recognized Miss Graylocke. The man, with whom she was so engrossed that she hadn't paid attention to her footing, was Lord Glendore. Both appeared to be in a world of their own making. As Wayland dropped his hand from around her waist, lingering for only a heartbeat longer than necessary to assure himself of her safety, Katherine smiled and watched the loving couple. Philomena must have passed along the information as Katherine had asked. It warmed her heart to see another happy ending.

She wasn't the only person taking note of Miss Graylocke's happiness. Unfortunately, Mrs. Fairchild had them in her sights as well.

"Katherine?"

She shook herself, returning to her conversation with her friends... and Wayland, who still stood close. Katherine checked her position before stepping back.

Pru said, "I asked if you've informed Lady Brackley of our findings. She *was* the person to point us in the direction of the case."

Katherine shook her head. "I was waiting to hear from Lyle before I gave her the final verdict. She'll undoubtedly want to talk to all of us in the coming few weeks and learn every minute detail of our investigations. She is writing another book, you know."

The men nodded emphatically and said in unison, "I've heard." They caught each other's eye and grimaced.

Pru beamed. "I cannot wait! She comes up with the most imaginative stories." Her smile fell away as she stared over Katherine's shoulder. Under her breath, Pru made a dismayed sound. "Katherine, I think Mrs. Fairchild wishes a word with you. She's coming this way."

Wayland spread his hands. "Shall I intercept her? I *am* supposed to make a fool of myself tonight."

Although Mrs. Fairchild had made Katherine's life difficult more than once, she shook her head. "I'll deal with her. I'm certain she won't have much to say."

In a sly voice, Pru added, "And you can hold up your end of the bargain." She tapped her fiancé on the shoulder.

Katherine lifted her face. "Oh? And what wager is this?"

Pru looked smug. "We couldn't let you and Captain Wayland have all the fun. So we made a little wager of our own. From now until the end of the Season—"

"Or our marriage," Lord Annandale grumbled.

Gracious, Pru inclined her head. "Or our marriage. Though perhaps I'll make you wait until the end of the Season."

He looked dismayed. "You would nae!"

Her expression softened. She trailed her finger over his sleeve, speaking softly. "You're right. I wouldn't. It won't be too much longer, my love. I promise."

Katherine cleared her throat. "The wager?"

"Oh, yes!" Pru dropped her hand. "Any time Lady Dalhousie comes over to speak with us, my Annandale must listen to her tales. *I* am allowed to find an excuse to be elsewhere."

She pushed at his shoulder, turning him toward the lady in question. With a forlorn sigh, he beseeched Wayland. "I don't suppose you'd come and keep a man company, would you?"

Wayland laughed and clapped him on the shoulder. "I suppose I might as well." They lumbered out of earshot. However, when Katherine strained her ears, she caught Lord Annandale's booming voice a moment later. "I see ye're wearing your famed necklace again, milady. I'd forgotten how you came by it. I don't suppose ye'd care to enlighten me again?"

Katherine practically heard Wayland grit his teeth. The lot of them had heard the embellished story of how Lady Dalhousie had come by her infamous necklace more times than they could count. If she wasn't set on changing the tale every time she recounted it, they could probably have recited it.

Katherine faced Mrs. Fairchild with Pru by her side.

"Lady Katherine, too good to see you."

Since she sounded as insincere as she looked, Katherine didn't bother saying the same. "You sound surprised. Why wouldn't I have come tonight? It is the ball of the season."

Mrs. Fairchild, dressed as Miss Romance, batted her hand through the air. "Why, I assumed you would know. Everyone read about your defeat this morning."

Katherine fought not to groan. "My defeat?"

"It's in the *Times*, of course. Miss Graylocke will be marrying the Earl of Glendore. What a shame you weren't able to secure that duke for her."

Katherine simply smiled. So everyone thought it was a defeat? All the better. Then maybe they would stop asking her to matchmake. "She prefers the earl."

Mrs. Fairchild waved her hand through the air. "Of course she does. Me? I snared *my* client a duke." She raised an eyebrow, a supercilious expression matched by the smirk curving one corner of her mouth. "I do wish you better luck next time."

Pru patted her on the arm, conciliatory. "She doesn't know what she's talking about. Your matches are far happier than hers, I'm sure."

Katherine laughed. "Since you're one of them, I'll count that as praise."

To avoid being asked to dance, she and Pru settled into two chairs in the corner, where they had a good vantage of the room, including the pained expressions on Lord Annandale and Wayland's faces as Lady Dalhousie continued her long-winded tale.

"Do you think he'll continue until summer?"

Pru laughed. "He's a steadfast sort of man. I think he might. But it won't be too much longer. A few weeks at most." She turned to Katherine with a gleam in her eye. "I've been thinking."

"Oh?" Katherine didn't like the look on her friend's face.

"I think we should join with the men for the next investigation."

With Wayland? Katherine fought the urge to look at the man in question, difficult to do when he was wearing so gaudy an outfit.

"We've already investigated with Lord Annandale. I don't object to his and McTavish's inclusion."

"And Captain Wayland?"

Katherine balled her fists on her knees. She didn't look Pru in the eye. Truth be told, she didn't know what to say. Wayland had been a constant in all of her investigations since she struck out from her father's side. She still didn't know why, except in this case when he had been working against her for the wager. The entire time, she'd assumed that he wanted information, wanted glory, wanted ... something. Then there was the matter of her father's disapproval. If she welcomed him into her investigations, she might not have the excuse of Lord Annandale to hide behind, as she had this time.

But she was her own woman, with her own judgments. Did she have to heed Papa's advice to stay clear of him?

"Think of all the good it will do," Pru cajoled. "They're every bit as adept as we are. I'm certain they were only a step or two behind us in this investigation. Plus, they can get information that we can't. Like at the club."

She did have a point...

Pru patted Katherine's knee. "And after I'm married, and we're in Scotland — not all year, but my Annandale has duties, and we'll want a honeymoon too, and..." She blushed. "While we're gone, you'll have someone to help investigate here."

Katherine twisted her mouth. "I have Harriet. I have Lyle."

"Harriet is your lady's maid. She has responsibilities of her own. As does Lyle."

Katherine made a face. "And Wayland does not?"

"His business *is* investigating. As is yours. He might be a useful man to keep close."

Katherine shook her head. "I've welcomed your help in these investigations, but I can solve crimes on my own."

Pru patted her arm. "Just you wait and see. On our next case, I think you might find that he's not as bad as you seem to think he is. Besides, it's dangerous investigating on your own. If I'm away, who will clobber murderers over the head?"

Katherine nearly rolled her eyes before she recalled where she was. "I'm not so helpless as that."

"I'm only saying you could use some help."

"But not from Wayland. Papa—"

Pru raised her eyebrows. "Who says your father needs to find out? You're buying the townhouse on Charles Street, aren't you? Unless you tell him, your father will never know who you keep company with. He's too busy preparing for the baby."

Pru had a point. And, if she was shortly to leave London, having another person to discuss ideas and formulate plans with might be a good idea. Katherine's gaze wandered to Wayland. As if he felt it, he lifted his eyes, and their gazes locked. He couldn't know her mind from this distance, nor she his, but he was an adept detective. Perhaps having his help wouldn't be the worst thing imaginable...

"I'll consider it, if he behaves."

He smiled at her, as unrepentant as ever.

****

MORE BOOKS in the Lady Katherine Regency Mystery series:

An Invitation to Murder (Book 1)
The Baffling Burglaries of Bath (Book 2)
Murder at the Ice Ball (Book 3)

SIGN up to join my email list to get all my latest release at the lowest possible price, plus as a benefit for signing up today, I will send you a copy of a Leighann Dobbs book that hasn't been published anywhere...yet!

http://www.leighanndobbs.com/newsletter

. . .

IF YOU ARE ON FACEBOOK, please join my VIP readers group and get exclusive content plus updates on all my books. It's a fun group where you can feel at home, ask questions and talk about your favorite reads:

https://www.facebook.com/groups/ldobbsreaders/

IF YOU WANT to receive a text message on your cell phone when I have a new release, text COZYMYS-TERY to 88202 (sorry, this only works for US cell phones!)

Lexy Baker Cozy Mystery Series Boxed Set Vol 1 (Books 1-4)

Or buy the books separately:

Killer Cupcakes

Dying For Danish

Murder, Money and Marzipan

3 Bodies and a Biscotti

Brownies, Bodies & Bad Guys

Bake, Battle & Roll

Wedded Blintz

Scones, Skulls & Scams

Ice Cream Murder

Mummified Meringues

Brutal Brulee (Novella)

No Scone Unturned

Cream Puff Killer

Kate Diamond Mystery Adventures

***

Hidden Agemda (Book 1)

Ancient Hiss Story (Book 2)

Heist Society (Book 3)

Silver Hollow

Paranormal Cozy Mystery Series

***

A Spell of Trouble (Book 1)

Spell Disaster (Book 2)

Nothing to Croak About (Book 3)

Cry Wolf (Book 4)

Mooseamuck Island

Cozy Mystery Series

* * *

A Zen For Murder

A Crabby Killer

A Treacherous Treasure

Mystic Notch

Cat Cozy Mystery Series

* * *

Ghostly Paws

A Spirited Tail

A Mew To A Kill

Paws and Effect

Probable Paws

Hazel Martin Historical Mystery Series

***

Murder at Lowry House (book 1)

Murder by Misunderstanding (book 2)

Lady Katherine Regency Mysteries

***

An Invitation to Murder (Book 1)

The Baffling Burglaries of Bath (Book 2)

Murder at the Ice Ball (Book 3)

A Murderous Affair (Book 4)

Too Close For Comfort

Regency Romance

* * *

Scandals and Spies Series:

Kissing The Enemy

Deceiving the Duke

Tempting the Rival

Charming the Spy

Pursuing the Traitor

Captivating the Captain

The Unexpected Series:

An Unexpected Proposal

An Unexpected Passion

Dobbs Fancytales:

Dobbs Fancytales Boxed Set Collection

Western Historical Romance

***

Goldwater Creek Mail Order Brides:

Faith

American Mail Order Brides Series:

Chevonne: Bride of Oklahoma

Magical Romance with a Touch of Mystery

***

Something Magical

Curiously Enchanted

ABOUT LEIGHANN DOBBS

USA Today bestselling author, Leighann Dobbs, discovered her passion for writing after a twenty year career as a software engineer. She lives in New Hampshire with her husband Bruce, their trusty Chihuahua mix Mojo and beautiful rescue cat, Kitty. When she's not reading, gardening, making jewelry or selling antiques, she likes to write cozy mystery and historical romance books.

Her book "Dead Wrong" won the "Best Mystery Romance" award at the 2014 Indie Romance Convention.

Her book "Ghostly Paws" was the 2015 Chanticleer Mystery & Mayhem First Place category winner in the Animal Mystery category.

Find out about her latest books by signing up at:

http://www.leighanndobbs.com/newsletter

Connect with Leighann on Facebook
http://facebook.com/leighanndobbsbooks

Join her VIP readers group on Facebook:
https://www.facebook.com/
groups/ldobbsreaders/

About Harmony Williams

If Harmony Williams had a time machine, she would live in the Regency era. The only thing she loves more than writing strong, funny women in polite society is immersing herself in the nuances of the past. When not writing or researching, she likes to binge-watch mystery shows and spend time with her one-hundred-pound lapdog in their rural Canadian home. For glimpses into the secrets and settings of future *Regency Matchmaker Mystery* books, sign up for her newsletter at http://www.harmonywilliams.com/newsletter.

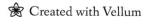